PU

NO P

'Pete Williams, macho hero of the future, you're on your all-conquering way with mucho aggro.'

Apathy rules OK with Pete Williams. He is quite happy to retreat from life into his bedroom with his punk music, his old comics and his animals. The day his O level results come through changes all this and Pete is determined to start his new VI form college as the new macho Pete Williams – with a renewed vigour for life and determined to stand on his own feet.

He becomes involved in an unlikely trendy group at college – a group which unfortunately includes the dubious Oliver and Kenny – and, as events escalate, Pete finds that he needs the support of his family and home more than he'd thought.

Written with humour and understanding, *No Place Like* is Gene Kemp's first book for teenagers.

NO PLACE LIKE
Gene Kemp

PUFFIN BOOKS
in association with
Faber and Faber

Puffin Books, Penguin Books Ltd, Harmondsworth, Middlesex, England
Viking Penguin Inc., 40 West 23rd Street, New York, New York 10010, U.S.A.
Penguin Books Australia Ltd, Ringwood, Victoria, Australia
Penguin Books Canada Ltd, 2801 John Street, Markham, Ontario, Canada L3R 1B4
Penguin Books (N.Z.) Ltd, 182–190 Wairau Road, Auckland 10, New Zealand

First published by Faber and Faber Limited 1983
Published in Puffin Books 1985

Printed and bound in Great Britain by
Cox & Wyman Ltd, Reading
Typeset in Bembo

For Judith

Thanks and acknowledgements are due to:—

Ted Hopkin, Head of English, Exeter College;
Bill Greenwell, English Department, Exeter College;
Dick Appleyard, Art and Design, Exeter College;
Freya Searle, President of the Students' Union 1981–1982;
Andrew Foss for his poem "Peter Moonfool";

and the coffee drinking lads.

PART ONE

◆

"Something better change."

1

When I was a little kid, about eleven, at Primary School, I remember the teacher talking to us one day about being afraid. He read a story to us out of the *Jungle Book* called "How Fear Came", and then a chapter from *The Hobbit*, where they make their way through those frightening woods. Next he read "Ghoolies and Ghosties" and a whole lot of scary poems and then got us to talk about what scared us, horror films or dentists, hairy great spiders or things lurking under the bed, being struck by lightning or diabolical monsters. I didn't say a thing, I don't much, even though ideas and words are hopping round like fleas in my head. That's where they stay. Locked up. I can't get them out. And there are so many things that give me the shivs that I couldn't possibly tell them all. Just thinking about them even there in the classroom was enough, and when Sir asked us to write a story or a poem about our own fears, then I knew there wasn't enough room in all the world to put down mine. So I doodled on my page, thinking about safe things like doughnuts or tortoises and waited for the morning to be over.

But my friend Nick went up to Sir in no time at all, clutching his paper and grinning all over his face as usual. Feeling curious I walked up to the desk as well, sticking out my neck to see what he'd written and it was,

"I'm afraid that Liverpool won't win the FA Cup this year."

Sir laughed. "Is that really all you're afraid of?"

"Yes," said Nick, "I didn't find those bits you read us a bit frightening."

"Lucky you. What have you written, Peter?"

"Nothing."

"You're not afraid of anything, either?"

"No, I'm scared of everything, even ordinary things."

"Oh, yes, sometimes it's the ordinary things that are the worst."

That Friday morning, years later, when I picked up the envelope addressed in my own handwriting and knew what the horrible thing contained and stood staring at it, like a rabbit hypnotized by a snake, then that far-off lesson flashed into my head for no reason at all, like a shot from an old film. Nick and I had split since then, going to different schools, but I knew somewhere he'd be opening his envelope with a flourish and laughing like a drain.

"For Heaven's sake get on with it and stop pithering about like an old hen," growled my father, slicing off the top of his boiled egg with millimetric accuracy.

Now don't get me wrong. I'm not scared of my Dad. He's a great guy. Besides, I've grown used to him. It's just that he's so much, if you know what I mean. He walks into a room and it's crowded.

I opened the envelope. It split all ways and the contents fluttered to the floor. I managed to get at them first, Dad being occupied with his runny yolk at the time.

So I read my results. I thought they'd be bad. They were worse. Silently I handed them over.

"It doesn't seem much to go out into the world with," he remarked gently. "One CSE grade Four in Metalwork. Just how many subjects did you take?"

"Eight." I waited.

There followed a very long and nasty silence while my father

10

stared at this little bit of paper as if it was going to grow into bank notes or something.

"I can see that. How come you made this exception for Metalwork? It spoils the straight run. Was it that it was so easy that even you couldn't screw it up? Or was your teacher some kind of genius?"

At that moment Ma came in, followed by my sister, Sal, all keen and eager to get at my results. When she'd seen them Ma sat down, looking green.

"I'll make a fresh pot of tea," Sal offered in a low voice as if we were at a funeral.

But Ma took a deep breath. "He's had a lot of problems, so I didn't expect miracles."

"That's just as well as you didn't get 'em, did you?" snapped Dad, doing terrible things to his toast. Sal moved her cup and plate to the sink unit to be out of range in case he really started firing. He did.

"Problems you call it," he shouted at Ma. "Just why don't you face up to the fact that your son has an IQ in single figures?"

Then he turned back to me.

"And what do you intend doing with your future? Have you any plans at all for when you leave school?"

He'd got on his silky voice, but it was clear to me that one of Dad's Inquisitions was about to begin. These always take place at meal times, and a lot of grub has been wrecked that way, like the Sunday lunch-time when he hit the plate with his fist, Yorkshire pud flew through the air and I ended up in the Eye Hospital. I stepped back a bit so that I was lined up behind Sal, who's bigger than I am anyway.

"I can always go on Social Security," I said, right out of the blue, nobody more amazed than me. There was a fearful black hole of a silence, then Ma started to rattle away like a machine gun.

"Now you know it's absolutely essential to pass some exams enough to get you to college or perhaps you could train . . ."

Dad's roar blasted through this like a landslide blotting out a small, pebbly path.

"You can get your bloomin' great feet under someone else's table then. That's what my Dad said to us lads. Work or get out!"

"Oh, not that boring old crap," cried Sal, glaring back at him. "That's all out of date. Gone. It's not the same for Pete. Nor any of us nowadays."

"It's not the same for him because he's bone, absolutely bone idle. He's always been bone idle. He always will be bone idle, God help me."

And Dad threw his mangled toast at the sink just missing her. We were well away now. I took a step towards the kitchen door, hellbent on escape.

But it was a waste of time.

"Listen To Me When I Talk To You. D'You Hear? I'm not having you hanging about the house like an under-used spare part."

"Dad. Listen. I'm not any good at anything. I keep telling people. But I don't want much, honest. I shan't cost you much. I don't have any ambition. Just to be left alone a bit."

Dad leapt in the air, shaking his fists at the ceiling and hitting it by accident, being a big man.

"Who on earth do you think doesn't want to be left alone? I know I do!" he cried and rushed out of the kitchen. Sal and I fell back against the sink unit.

"I'm making some coffee," Sal said. "I need it."

Ma seemed to have recovered and was making plans; she's like that.

"You're already registered at the Sixth Form College so you can retake your exams there."

"Perhaps they won't have me now," I said hopefully. I

hated the sound of the Sixth Form College, despite everyone telling me it was great. She took no notice anyway.

"It's a very good place and I'm sure they'll be able to do something with you. I did anticipate that you'd be doing your A Levels there but we shall have to see."

"I don't much want to take those exams again, Ma."

"Don't call me Ma. I've asked you time and time again. It makes me sound like one of those awful women pioneers in petticoats and a wagon trail. Either call me mother or Margaret. Even Maggie would do. But not Ma. That's settled then, Peter. I see no difficulties about your being able to retake your exams and get a good result. The Principal, Wreford Partridge, is an old friend of mine, and he's already well acquainted with your problems."

Sal and I groaned. "Our problem is the word problem," Sal had once shouted at one of Ma's awful coffee mornings when the word was on all coffee-drinking lips.

Dad loomed in the doorway.

"You. Listen. I don't care if you get fifty degrees as your mother would like, or whether you go down the mines or deep-sea fishing as I suggest. It's not important. What is important is that you get it firmly into your thick head that you are not going to be hanging round this house all day long lying on your bed and listening to your diabolical music while I am grafting away to maintain you in idle comfort. IS THAT CLEAR?"

His voice rang out like a bell in a broom cupboard.

"I've got it clear, Dad," I agreed, nodding up and down Japanese style.

He banged out of the house like a bout of bad weather. Ma continued,

"Sal's done well at the college. So did Mike."

"But I'm me. Pete. Remember?"

"Let me finish," she said.

13

"There's no way of stopping you," sighed Sal and she was right. Ma went rabbiting on.

"I'll see Wreford Partridge and discuss your problems and arrange a course for you."

Shame, rage and despair scalded through my veins at the vile prospect of me and my problems being stretched out in front of this Partridge bloke like a drain with its cover off.

"I don't think I'll pass those exams if I take them over and over again."

She didn't hear me. "I shall have to go now," she said. "That's settled then."

When she'd gone Sal made some more coffee.

"You are a twit," she said, but amiably. "You only needed to pass a couple just to keep them happy. It's easy to pass silly old exams."

"You're different."

"I know," she said and we sat listening to the radio till it was time for her to go fish-frying at the Batter Plaice.

"What an unfortunate name," Ma said when she first got the job.

"Serve up battered wives, do they?" Dad chortled, asking for trouble and getting it.

"That, Colin, is not funny," Ma said and to prove it served up burnt fish fingers and bullet-hard yellow peas for two days running, followed by Toad-in-the-Hole, one of the world's great worst dishes. My room was deep in chip wrappers except when I could afford Kentucky Fry.

2

After Sal had gone I switched off the door bell so that I shouldn't have to answer the door, then took the phone off the hook. I didn't feel like talking to anyone. I did think about ringing my friend Willie Trent, to see if he'd managed to do worse than I had, but he'd be bound to appear for he turned up at some time or other every day. Right at that moment I needed the security of my room, where things had been the same for a very long time, like the elderly blackamoor fish and two antique gerbils. One of them, Bert, could only just get up his little ladder, for he'd got arthritis in his back legs. Posters were peeling off the walls and the curtains had Noddy on them so they must have hung there for ages. I'd got records and cassettes and collections of comics piled everywhere. People told me they were appreciating in value but I just liked having them there along with old skateboards, old radios, old cameras and a whole load of Dinky toys. There I felt safe. I'd pulled round the bookcase so I could lie in bed with books at hand and my cassette player and not be seen from the doorway. Here was my space. A cavern of books and bits.

I put on an old punk recording just right for the way I felt that day, and sank down into the bed and down into the music which took me and carried me away into wild space and the sound of the universe, where I could be free and untouched by people, be alone unto myself and unafraid.

I must have fallen asleep for I came to suddenly woken by the sound not of the universe but loud banging and roaring going on somewhere. I heaved myself off the bed in time to see Dad filling the doorway. Speaking.

"I come home early," he was saying in a voice loud even for him, "having spent my lunch-time beavering away on your behalf . . ."

"You needn't have bothered . . ." I began and then sniffed the air.

"Dad, what's that terrible smell?"

My father did a dance up and down in the doorway. For a big man he's light on his feet.

"Aha, so you noticed, did you? You're quick, I'll say that for you. In fact you amaze me. I never fail to be amazed at you through life, but today you have surpassed even yourself. 'What's that smell?' you ask, standing there like a great goop. That smell, my boy, is the smell of the house burning."

"The house burning?"

"You heard me. That's what I said. And you understood, did you? Clever boy."

I managed to peer past him to a blue and smoke-filled landing. A strong pong of grilled grill was floating up the stairs.

"Hadn't we better do something?" I tried to push past him.

"Don't worry," he said soothingly. "It's all under control. But only because," his voice started to get louder until it beat into my skull like hammer blows, "I arrived home early full of peace and good will towards men, to find what? What indeed?" he bellowed, lowering his face close to mine. "You might well ask. Half a dozen people crowding round the front door, its bell out of action, telephone engineers trampling all over the garden because the line's been reported out of order, and a fire engine screeching to a halt outside the house. Didn't you even hear that?"

I shook my head.

16

"The kitchen full of smoke and about to burst into flames!"
I tried to speak and couldn't.

"But don't worry about it. Don't give it a thought. It was just someone who shall be nameless, had left the grill on with toast under it, or what had been toast in earlier times . . ."

Oh, no, now I remembered.

"We were lucky the old bat next door noticed the smoke, tried to do something, found she couldn't get in and rang the fire brigade which is when I arrived, and I don't mean old bat, I mean dear old soul."

"Is it all right? Is there much damage?"

"Not so much damage as I'd like to do to you, you incompetent nincompoop. The kitchen is greasy and smoky and filthy, the ceiling is black, the whole house reeks and the grill will never be the same again, but don't worry, it's all right, the house hasn't actually burnt down. We still have a roof over our heads. And I'm so glad you got in a good morning's zizz, so essential to growing lads, because you're going to need all that energy for washing down walls and cleaning up. One thing, we don't need Job Creation Schemes with you around, do we?"

That last bit made him happy and he stopped dancing about and then I knew the worst was over. There wasn't really anything I could say except to mutter sorry which got swallowed up by him roaring suddenly,

"What have you got to say?"

"Dad, let me past. I'm bursting."

His cry of despair followed me to the bathroom. When I got back he was still talking.

"Tell me how can such things be? I know some mothers do 'ave 'em but this is ridiculous. Just how did I ever come to have you? I can't have been that bad, surely? I'm not what you'd call a good man, I've never claimed that, but how I ever got you is a mystery to me. The milkman, I wonder? No, your mother is a woman of high principles if nothing else. Besides I don't

17

think he fancies her. She is not a pretty woman. But I do blame your mother, I do indeed. Your stupidity, your laziness, your incompetence, your sheer lack of any know-how whatsoever, your . . ."

"Absolutely right, Dad," I said, getting in a word. "Don't worry about it."

"Oh, go and do something useful. Like getting stuck into the kitchen."

Much later, when the clearing up was done and my father had simmered down and cheered up, we played Penalty, a board game. He's a great games player and was winning as usual. Some day I might beat him and then I'll jump through the ceiling, but it wasn't likely on that day which had been one of my all-time losers. Suddenly he looked up and said,

"Oh, by the way, I ran into your mother in town as I do from time to time much as I try to avoid it and she told me she's already seen the Weevil Bird or whatever his name is and he'll be keeping an eye on you, his third presumably, as he must be using the other two in the ordinary course of the day. What are you twitching for?"

Twitching? It was enough to make anyone twitch. How could she? How dare she? I could just hear my mother saying, well you know, Wreford, he's got such problems. I wanted to lie down on the floor, beat with my hands, kick with my feet, and scream, and scream. I loathed knowing people were discussing me, saying things about me. I didn't much want to go to the College. I didn't want to take my exams again, but if I could do it without any notice being taken I could just about bear it. Why should I be treated like a ten-year-old? It was my life, wasn't it? Even if I didn't have much clue how to manage it. I'd never get the hang of it at this rate. Suddenly I wanted to have the guts to pick up the board, hurl it across the room, tear out of the house and spend the rest of the summer hitch-hiking

18

round the country, living by busking and on my wits. The trouble was I can't sing and I don't appear to have much in the way of wits. So everybody says. And I'm scared of everything like I told you.

"Here, try to concentrate your mind a bit. If you have one to concentrate, that is. Or you'll lose this game as well."

"I don't care," I muttered, but he didn't hear. We went on playing. After a while he said,

"Lucky old you having parents who take an interest in you. My old man never took a blind bit of notice of me. Don't think he'd have recognized me if he'd seen me in the street, not that he recognized anyone much in the condition he was usually in. Still, it wasn't surprising. We were a terrible bunch of kids, your uncles and I."

Lucky? You were the lucky one. You were left alone, hidden among that crowd of brothers. You lot were able to be a cheery gang of villains in peace. You weren't watched and noticed and criticized all the time.

A strange wild song by a group who were later nearly all killed in a plane crash rang through my head, an old song telling of things I feel. I jumped up and ran out of the room, away from the game that I was losing, away from my father, talking, talking, double talking. I'd escape somewhere, find freedom, be free as a bird. The front door was open. The summer night lay before me. I was going into it.

Following the fire engine the gas engineers had arrived in the road. They had dug a trench and surrounded it by warning lights, only they didn't warn me, my head being too full of the night and music and rebellion to see what was before me. I tripped straight over one and fell into the trench. The day that had begun badly and got worse as it went along folded me up into blackness.

My father was carrying me up the stairs, speaking as he did so.

Somewhere far off I could hear Ma saying Pete and problems.

"Just think," Dad said. "I used to do this when he was a baby and I'm still doing it."

I tried to struggle up and out and banged into the bookcase at the side of my bed where Dad was dumping me. It was all I needed. Was there no escape? Death, where is thy sting? (I used to be a choirboy till they threw me out for not being able to sing on the note.) As I collapsed on the bed, I thought this had got to change. This has just got to change.

Pete Williams, macho hero of the future, you're on your all-conquering way. With mucho aggro.

Oh, my poor head.

3

A giant pterodactyl flapped behind me uttering antediluvian cries as I ran at action replay speed across a ploughed field of glue growing Biros with grinning poppy heads. "The Weevil Bird," I cried and woke to find Dad beside the bed, clutching a mug of tea which he thrust at me, so that I had to haul myself up fast before I was deluged. My head ached and I had a strange feeling that I'd solved something but I couldn't remember what.

"What's the time?"

"Half past six."

"Oerh," I groaned, feeling weak. "What you doin' up at this time, Dad?"

He was looking round the room in a feverish fashion, but jerked back when I said that.

"Me? Oh, I'm off to London by early train, and I just wanted to check that you hadn't died overnight, and I see you haven't, though that astonishes me since I can't see that it's possible to spend a night in this vile and disgusting room without catching plague."

"It's not bad, Dad. I like it."

"Not bad! It's appalling. Look at that pile of dirty socks. Look at that heap of rotting comics. Smell the air, boy, or rather don't, or you will probably be asphyxiated as I almost was when I was misguided enough to set foot in here this morning. It's like a compost heap. But perhaps you've got used to it."

21

I put the tea down, lay back and closed my eyes. Almost, I preferred the pterodactyl. Suddenly he bent down.

"What are all these rusty nails doing scattered over the floor? Are you studying to be an Indian fakir? Your mother has always hoped you'd study something. Can this be it, one asks?"

"A what?" I asked, giving up hope of sleep.

"An Indian fakir. They lie on nails for fun and religious principles."

He was now dancing round the bin. Why wasn't he old and tired like other fathers? Or like me, for that matter?

"Are you growing penicillin in here, then? Or pot, maybe? Whatever it is it's doing well. I bet it could nearly walk itself to the dustbin. Why don't you train it? I've no doubt a spot of bin-training could become fascinating given time. It could become a career."

Bert had emerged into a geriatric morning.

"Are those animals still alive? I remember giving them to you in a fit of madness on your fifth birthday. Why don't they die decently like other people's pets?"

"They're different ones, Dad. They're not that old."

I put down the stewed tea and slid under the bedclothes, for there was no answer to my father. Arguing with him is like arguing with the forces of Nature, too much for me. He placed himself at the foot of the bed, addressing me like addressing a meeting, but then, he's always addressing meetings. I shall never, never go to a meeting as long as I live, in fact, the life of a walled-in hermit would suit me right now.

"When I am away I want you to get the kitchen ready for decorating, and while you're doing that you may as well clear out this room, strip down the walls and then we can do this one as well before you start at the College. I shall look forward to it. Enjoy yourself. Cheers."

I pulled the sheet right over my head and sank into oblivion.

"This is a peace house" it says on our front door, don't laugh. When Sal saw it she said, "Who needs nukes? We got Dad." Ma is always putting up stickers and things like that. She had a strict childhood up north, she says, where they went to chapel all the time except when she was at a very academic school where they did Latin and Science and a spot of Greek for fun on Friday afternoons. Then she shocked everybody by running off with Dad, who was married with one son Mike, yuck, came south, had me and Sal, and got stuck into CND, Friends of the Earth, Transport 2000, you name it, Ma supports it. She also teaches and wrote a book called *Class Control*, which operates on a lot of different levels apparently and created quite a stir. I wouldn't know as I don't intend reading it.

Sal was brewing up in the kitchen with Willie when I eventually got up. He'd managed two CSEs and an O Level and was pleased with himself, in any case he's always happy when Sal's around for he fancies her no end. Lots of people do as she takes after Dad but is in better shape. Willie's really my only friend, a human stick insect, getting thinner as he grows taller and taller, like pastry being rolled out. He's got the skinniest legs in the narrowest jeans I've ever seen and believes that the human race is in the process of becoming God. What about Hitler I ask but he never answers. He rabbits on about the universe a lot, black holes and quasars and pulsars, and sometimes this is interesting and sometimes not, for old Willie does get a bit boring.

"What a smashing lump you've got there," he said.

"Dad said he thought you'd gone completely off your rocker instead of only partly, and tried to commit suicide in a trench. Silly old Pete, nothing's that bad," Sal said.

"I didn't try to do myself in. I just got fed up, that's all. I think I was trying to run away."

"I'll help you organize it better next time."

"I can do it myself, thanks. I wish everyone would stop trying to run me and my life."

"Sorry, sorry. Didn't know you were feeling stroppy."

"I'm not. It's just that everyone gets at me and makes me feel useless."

"I don't," they both said at the same time.

"No, not you two. But everybody else does. And even you do a bit, Sal. How would you like to have Sara the Wonder Horse around all the time? Six foot two, eyes of blue, see what Super Sara can do?"

"That's not fair. And my eyes are brown, not blue."

"Look at it from my point of view. There you are, dripping with O and A Levels, passed your driving test first go, Head Girl at school, next year's President of the Students' Union. Whereas me, I've never been able to do anything. Remember when I got into the football team at last, and sprained my ankle in the first match and had to be carried off . . . and when I was in the school play and fell off the stage by accident and the audience rolled in the aisles . . . ?"

"Yes, it was hilarious," Sal grinned.

"No, it wasn't. It was a very serious, historical play."

"Poor Pete."

"Oh, leave it, leave it. I tell you I'm not gonna be poor Pete much longer. I'm sick of being pushed around, everybody's second-rate citizen. I'm gonna . . ."

But I never told them what I was going to do for at that moment Aunt Sybil arrived in the kitchen with Ma. She raised her eyes at Willie, who was wearing his sister's Afghan coat with the sleeves cut out and his new ear-rings. Aunt Sybil always makes him very nervous — she makes everyone very nervous — and he dropped his little herbal ciggie (he rolls them out of dried dandelions, I think, and they're vile, just vile), picked it up and stubbed it out on the new loaf Ma had just put down. Aunt Sybil started to cough and wave her silk handkerchief about.

"Do they have to look like that, Margaret?" she asked,

absolute cheek because she was sporting her razor-edged trousers and a shirt covered with whips and chains and hunting crops. You felt you'd get slashed if you got anywhere near. Dad says she makes Attila the Hun look like a member of the SDP, and always goes out the moment she appears. Actually Ma can't stand her either but she is her sister so she feels she has to put up with her.

"How did you get on with your exams, Willie?" she asked, trying to change the subject, but by now Willie was oozing backwards out of the kitchen and down the hall.

"Oh, oh, very nicely, thank you very much," and he waved like the Queen Mother, a terrified look on his face. I started to ooze after him as Aunt Sybil cried,

"You didn't do much, did you, Peter? Your mother's very disappointed and I'm not surprised. But the youth of today doesn't want to work that's what I think. In my day we had to buckle down and get our noses to the grindstone . . ."

"You must have looked most peculiar," Sal smiled sweetly. Aunt Sybil stopped, looked at her suspiciously, then murmured,

"Dear Sara. Always so witty. Such a good girl." She's never realized that her dear Sara takes the mickey out of her most of the time. But I'd heard enough, and I speeded up so much I landed on Willie's size fourteens. He gave a loud hooch of pain and on that note we both escaped.

"We'll soon have it finished," said my father. He had returned home filled with energy, ready to attack the house and everything else, me included. I doubted if we'd ever finish. Never had I seen such a mess in the whole of my life. In fact there it was, my life, which Dad had seized and thrown out into the skip, my sixteen years of old books, old records, old games and old toys. All my security had been taken away at one blow, gone for ever. The animals had been removed to the outside world of the upstairs landing and I doubted if Bert would ever be the same again. What really annoyed me was that it wasn't necessary. There was no need to waste time and money and energy on changing a room that was completely OK as it was. I tried to say this to my father but he only cried,

"Go and mix some Polyfilla. We're going to need lots of it."

It was all a terrible waste but there was no stopping him. He stood there like an earth-mover, a giant robot programming me into more and further activity, stripping my life away.

I ached. My hair and nose and eyes and mouth were full of bits as I laboriously pulled off the wallpaper, which had a railway engine pattern dating from when I was about eight. Dust, debris, dirt and water swirled about us. If I paused for a moment Dad would yell,

"Stop reading that comic and get on with it,"
as he stood naked to the waist wreathed in ringletting wallpaper strips, looking like a grey Incredible Hulk. From time to time when she wasn't fish-frying Sal would come in and help, and sometimes Willie, though after he knocked over a bucket of water Dad banned him for twenty-four hours, sending him for supplies of paint, etc., instead.

"It's bad over there. Where that fungus flourishes. We'll have to remove the old plaster. Someone's used the wrong kind. We'll start again with a fresh lot."

"Do we have to?" I asked and got a glare in return.

"If you think I'm enjoying this, you're wrong. Go and fetch the spade."

"Where from?"

He danced up and down a bit causing plaster to fall in large lumps.

"The shed, of course. Where d'you think I keep it? In the bathroom?"

I went into the garden, found the spade, then heard Aunt

26

Sybil's pseudo-county accents floating down the hall,

"I'm only dropping in for a moment, Margaret darling
. . ." and fled upstairs.

"I want to get on with this quickly," Dad said, "so you
knock that plaster off while I fill in over here."

"What do I have to do?" I hadn't a clue. He sighed heavily,
and picked up the spade.

"Just hold it like this and knock off the old, loose plaster."

The spade was heavy so I put all my force behind it and sliced
at the wall as Dad had shown me. There was a loud tearing
noise and the spade seemed to accelerate, taking me with it,
breaking through the wall, fragments flying, through something that crack-cracked like a machine gun, while the momen-
tum carried me forward through the collapsing, widening hole
into the room on the other side.

It was the bathroom. And there enthroned sat Aunt Sybil,
her face a few inches from mine, her mouth fixed in a never-
ending silent scream. A broken tile toppled into her lap as a
piece of plaster fell off my head. This gave her voice. Her
screams were blood-curdling. Dad hauled me back into my
room by my legs as Ma and Sal rushed upstairs and pounded on
the door.

Hours later, most of the mess cleared, and Dad at last not
speaking, I lay in my room listening to the Stones.

Sal slid in, bearing a huge packet of leftovers from the Batter
Plaice, sausages, skate, chicken and chips and gribbles.

"You get an awful lot," I said.

"Der Big Boss Man fancies me, that's why." She looked at
me slyly. "You'll find it funny later."

"You mean . . . Aunt Sybil . . ."

"I find it funny now," and we started to laugh and laugh
and laugh till Bert came out to peer at what was going on.

After a time she said, "What I really came in to tell you is I'm moving out."

"What?"

"I've got a flat. Prue Lennox has asked me to share with her and I thought I would. After all, I'm eighteen now and I think it's time I made a move. Leave the little ole nest an' all that."

"It'll be weird without you." I didn't know how I felt. "Who'll tell Dad what I'm trying to say?"

"You. It's time you did. He's a great guy when you've squared up to him."

"If I ever do."

"You will. It's a new start for you, too. College and all that. You might like it. I did. Not like school. Give it a whirl, Pete."

"Yeh. It's all changing — even my room. Dad's settled that all right. It'll never be the same."

"Good. Get out of it every now and then, instead of lying here brooding for days. Go and find what it's all about. Get yourself a girl."

"I don't know any girls. I don't know anybody, only Willie."

"Your life can only get better then, because it must be on the lowest possible level now. Here, have these last few gribbles."

I thought about telling her about the new macho Pete Williams, then changed my mind. After all there hadn't been any signs of him yet, so I'd wait. And show 'em. I hoped. But I was still scared. It could easily be dark outside.

PART TWO

"It was a gas."

1

Since I didn't have to wake up early on the first day of term naturally I woke up at two o'clock, three o'clock, four o'clock and so on and was just dropping off nicely when Willie appeared at eight wearing a tee shirt with RATS on it and carrying a brand new leather suitcase bearing his initials.

I peered through the sleep in my eyes and groaned.

"Where did you get that?"

"My Gran. She thinks I've made it to the top and got it specially for me."

"She's all right, your Gran."

"I know. That makes it worse. Where shall I hide it?"

"Under the bed."

We located a couple of polythene carriers, dug out two biros, a bit inky but still working, and so equipped we went for breakfast. Sal was already lashing up coffee and toast, still wearing her night tee shirt, which caused Willie to grow cross-eyed and drool alarmingly. She was sorting through millions of papers as she ate. She'd already been into College during the week and was humming with energy like a power house. Like Dad.

"You will come back here sometimes, won't you?" asked Willie, sounding pathetic, which he is, anyway.

"Yes, I'm only just round the corner. You'll be sick of the sight of me. Tell you what, Willie, we'll have a house-warming party and you shall both come. And meet some girls."

"I don't care about other girls," said Willie, at which Sal shot him a horrified look — I don't think she'd realized he was bats about her.

"Seems funny to see you two in jeans and not school uniform," she said in an over-forty voice, putting him in his place.

"Spare us. Please."

"You always had mash on the blazers."

"We threw the school dinners at each other."

"All they were fit for. The mash and the blazers."

Willie hung around waiting for Sal, but I had no intention of entering the place holding Big Sister's hand thank you very much. I'd done that at the Primary, Ma being too busy to take me, and it was years before they stopped calling me Sara Williams's little brother.

I was muttering mucho aggro, mucho aggro over and over again under my breath as a mantra to defend me against all the horrible things that I knew only too well could go wrong that day, or any other day, but especially that one. I'd made lots of resolutions about being relaxed, keeping calm, not flapping, easy, easy, laid back Pete, etc. I just wished my hands would stop trembling. Willie seemed happy enough. He looked mad but then he always does. He started to whistle.

"Shut up," I said.

"They say there are seven thousand students," he said brightly.

"Shut up," I said.

Yet his words struck me. Seven thousand. I'd forgotten there were that many. Surely I could camouflage myself among that lot and not be noticed. Operation for survival. A ship passing unseen in the night. Pete Williams come and gone. That would be easier than mucho aggro. And I was more used to it. Especially I'd like to be camouflaged against the watching eye of Wreford Partridge. I didn't think meeting him would do anything at all for either of us.

The Tower Block came into sight. Here we go. Into the conveyor belt of Education.

We were just in the entrance hall when a hand struck me from behind with such power that my knees buckled and oh, Lord, it's the Weevil Bird, I thought for one vile moment as I sank to the floor which wasn't at all the way I'd wanted to enter the place.

"Pete, me old mate," bellowed a voice above me as I struggled upwards to find my face at chest level with the dim and distant past.

"Nick," I bellowed back and my voice rose in a falsetto squeak which it never does nowadays except when you least want it to, like when meeting an old friend you remember being your size and who is now six miles high, taller even than Willie. At that moment a pair of arms wrapped themselves round my neck, from behind again. This time my knees didn't buckle, they trembled instead. The arms were very soft and cool.

"It's Peterkin, dear little Peterkin. Oh, how super to see you. Fancy you being here, but of course you would be. What's the matter? Don't you remember me?"

I unwrapped the arms and looked for somewhere to place my back out of danger. The owner of the arms cooed at me with a voice like velvet in honey, and I looked at her and looked away again. She was all too much. No one had any right to look like that. And the Comprehensive Willie and I attended was for boys only, remember (and all the things Ma said didn't change it while I was there). She'd turned out all gold and tawny, tawny hair, golden skin, golden eyes. She made me feel so dizzy I couldn't remember whether I remembered her or not, so I rummaged about in my head and came up with,

31

"You must have changed more than I have,"
which I thought was brilliant.

"Verna. Surely you remember now."

"Sure. We used to play together . . . when we were little
. . . then you moved away . . . you hit me with a spade
because you didn't want to go . . ."

"Try playing with her now she's big and see if she hits you
with a spade. Hi, Verna." Nick was moving in, of course.

The golden eyes shrivelled him. "I might have known
you'd be here."

"I'm Willie," said my friend.

"You must be joking," Nick grinned. Willie shot him a
look of hatred.

"I'm so glad you're here," Verna cried, beaming at me
with her American-type wrap-around teeth. "Remember the
fun we had in old Warty Jackson's class?"

"You bet he does," Nick said.

"A lot of our old class is here," went on Verna, taking no
notice of Nick. She certainly didn't seem to care for him
much.

"So's nearly everyone else's class," said Verna's mate, who
hadn't spoken up till now. She was a big girl, wearing a long
white shirt, striped football socks and striped hair.

"Meet Claire," said Verna. "Claire, here's Nick, he's horrible, I warn you, and Willie, Willie's sweet . . ." He
blushed scarlet ". . . and dear, dear little Peterkin. I shall look
after Peterkin. I always did."

Mucho aggro, mucho aggro I muttered under my breath.

"I don't like being called Peterkin," I said, but no one took
any notice.

"I don't like being called Willie," he said. Everybody
looked at him.

"No, I wouldn't like it either," said Claire gloomily. She
seemed a pretty gloomy girl.

"Then you shan't be. We'll give you another name. Carl. That's it. We'll call you Carl."

"I like that," beamed Willie, I mean Carl.

I looked around.

The entrance hall was full of students coming and going, some with not a clue in their heads as to what it was all about, like me, and others shouting and showing off to show how clued they were. Cries of I'm with Ted, old Josh, Liberal Arts, imagine old Scrimshaw doing that, four As, Cambridge, failed the whole lot, doing a ton, Social Security, Tamsin Shaw, really, problems, published, absolutely stoned, faculty, schedule, communications, pregnant, timetable, business studies, Science, Oxbridge, catering, disciplines, failed, Sara Williams, oh, you mean that Sara Williams.

Sara Williams passed by at that moment, surrounded by people. I shrank back and she didn't see me. But Nick saw her.

"Oh, yes, you're her brother aren't you? That's interesting."

"She's gorgeous," Willie said. "Oh, this is great, man," looking around and beaming. But my stomach had settled in a low aching position. What on earth was the matter with me? Everyone around looked happy or interested in what was going on. But given a straight choice I'd rather have been on a desert island or in a prehistoric cave with a sabre tooth on the prowl outside. What was I doing here? The rest looked confident as if they knew what to do, how to pick the right options, avoid trouble and the Weevil Bird.

"Don't worry," Verna whispered in my ear, causing it to wiggle. "It'll be all right, you'll see."

Somehow I didn't want Verna making my ears wiggle. All I wanted to do was slip away silently and lie on my bed listening to music. I was bewildered with all these people and the thought of what I'd have to cope with and I was no good at coping with places like this. The Comp. I went to seemed enormous till I got used to it and this place was much, much larger. I shrank back against a door and as I did so I caught sight of a girl's face very briefly, a funny sort of face, not glamorous at all, a bit crumpled and unhappy. "That one's even more miserable than I am," I thought, as the door behind me opened and I fell backwards on to a woman coming out carrying a pile of books. Out of control I skidded on to the books, which flew into the air, a heavy hardback shooting straight on to the face of a shortish, balding man with a big chin and hairy tweeds who had popped out of nowhere. Some part of me registered that I'd seen him before somewhere, and then I forgot that as his glasses fell to the floor and in the hush following my unbalancing act I could see they weren't broken, relief all round.

"I'm awfully sorry," I stammered, bending forward to pick them up and with the accuracy of a world class snooker player potting the pink and then the black I stepped first on one lens and then on the other. It was a difficult thing to do but I did it perfectly. They were shattered. Trembling I tried to rescue the remains but my fingers began to bleed.

"Don't bother," said the owner in a voice like a harsh northern winter. "I don't think they're worth it. What's your name? I've seen you before."

"Williams," I gulped as the entire entrance hall fell into rapturous silence and listened. No one moved. Nothing sounded. I fought back a mad urge to say Humphrey Bogart. "Peter Williams."

Students started to pick up the books and time started again.

"Are you all right?" asked the woman. She wasn't speaking to me.

"Of course I'm all right. See that this mess gets cleared up, please, and give my wife a ring to bring in a spare pair of glasses if she can. As for you, I've seen you about, when I've visited your mother. And there was no need for you to take this keeping an eye on you so seriously as to sabotage my specs.

34

After all, with any luck, we may never encounter one another again.''

And he was gone.

''Who was that?'' cried Willie. ''He seemed to know you.''

Several second-year students who'd been watching with great joy told him.

''I've never seen old Partridge so mad,'' said one, grinning from ear to ear.

''I think I'm really gonna like this place, man,'' said Nick.

''Poor Peterkin,'' murmured Verna.

''Tough,'' said Claire, smiling at last.

I just concentrated on my bleeding fingers.

2

I couldn't concentrate on the Principal's speech of welcome in the main hall, which wasn't surprising. Sal told me later that it was much better than usual, as he just spoke instead of reading from notes. His glasses hadn't arrived by then, apparently. I found afterwards that I hadn't the faintest idea what he'd said. But I've always been very good at not listening. I think it was the long assemblies we had in Primary School. It all went in at one ear and out the other, and after a time it became a habit and might be one of the reasons my results weren't up to much.

Afterwards, "Coffee," said Verna. "Let's all have coffee. Come along, Peterkin."

We trooped along to the coffee bar, Verna seeming to know where it was which is more than I did. The Tower Block, new glass and concrete, was surrounded by older buildings and huts, and the oldest hut, very grotty indeed, was the coffee bar. We went in, me trying to hide between Nick and Willie in case anyone recognized me as the Specs Breaker. Nick cleared a corner for us and we took a look round. There was a long queue at the bar and stretching outside. I could see lots of machines, Space Invaders, Phoenix, Defender, Gorf, Sting and Asteroids. It was a far cry from Rolleston Boys' Comprehensive.

"I'll get the coffee with Willie, I mean Carl. You stay there and keep the places," said Claire. There was a faint look of terror on his face but she led him away. Someone drifted up to our table and said to me, "Hey, you were brilliant. Can I get you anything?"

"No," I said, weakly.

"I will, anyway," he said and wandered away.

Two guys finished a game at the Phoenix next to us and came over. One had a narrow face and dark hair, the other, though not as tall as Nick, was built like a cross between a tank and Neanderthal Man.

"Hi, Nick," said the first.

"Hi."

"Who's the Joker, then?" he asked, indicating me. "You were great. Best performance I've seen here, yet."

"Wasn't he terrific?" said Verna proudly.

It seemed to me amazing that in a place with seven thousand students so many had seen me in action, for lots of nudges and grins were going on. Surely they weren't all in the hall at that particular moment, were they?

"This is Pete," said Nick. "And Willie, who's also called Carl, and is busy spilling the coffee. Claire. And Verna, the College's answer to Miss Universe. You'll find her quite universal."

"Shut up," she said. "Some people are handsome, some are nice, some are funny. Just try being one of them."

Claire was eating her way through the third Crunchie.

"Meet Oliver. He doesn't appear to have any other names. He was at school with me but further up, being a clever git. And Kenny, known as the Animal to all his friends but there aren't many of them. He wasn't at school with us."

"You're the public school crowd," put in Willie. "Why d'you come here, Nick, since you got your own Sixth Form?"

"My old man thought there'd be more opportunities here."

"For all sorts of things," murmured Oliver.

"What about Kenny?"

37

"What about me?"

"Oh, he's public school, too," grinned Oliver. "Borstal."

"If you're second year, what's this place like?" asked Willie.

"That's something you'll have to find out for yourself. I can only say there's no place like it."

Coffee and coke arrived for me.

"If you don't want it, I'll have it," Claire offered.

"Your sister's come in," Verna said. "Peterkin, be an angel and take me over to her. I've got something to ask her."

"No, if you want to speak to her do it yourself. Sorry, but I'm not going near Sal if I can help it. Not here."

"So you're the brother of the lovely Sara, are you?" said Oliver, not much he misses. "I'd like to meet her."

"She's not living at home now," I replied and then we started to move as word came round that we had to register and sign up. Only later did I wonder why I lied, then the music washed the thought and the day far away as I lay on my bed at peace, at last.

"Are you stone deaf as well as tone deaf?" roared my father from the doorway. "Turn down that appalling din. I can hear it from the other end of the house."

It's a pity he has no appreciation of good music.

3

Somehow we got settled in. After the ghastly and awful Weevil Bird beginning I managed to surface and started to find my way around the College, drank coffee, talked to people, played the machines, sorted out my timetable, acquired books, files and stationery and found, astonished, that I was still in one piece at the end of the day. On Day Two Willie and I set off for the annexe of the Liberal Arts Department where we'd be doing English Lang. and Lit. I was not looking forward to it for at Rolleston Comp. for Boys nothing had been more boring than Eng. Lang. which was always handed out in huge slabs of double period time at some part of the day such as Friday afternoon when you'd rather be doing something else or nothing else, but not comprehension, grammar and précis, varied by précis, grammar and comprehension. As for novels or poems, I hadn't seen or heard a poem since I was at the Primary School. Literature was wet and if you liked it you were in danger of being known as a poofter, Rolleston being noted for its rugger and little else. Football, which I wasn't bad at, was despised as being a game for the proles, although having changed to a Comp. from a Grammar School it really was now a school for the proles. Poetry, drama, dancing caused great falling and rolling about in massive paroxysms of mirth. I didn't suppose it would be any different here not that I cared and muttered mucho aggro to myself a few times to keep the spirits up as Willie and I followed a twisting lane lined with spiky railings that led up and down hills, past factories and schools and a church with a tall spire, past warehouses and a large stretch of BR property. The route was such a twister that we began to have doubts.

"We're going to be late, we should have given ourselves more time to get there," said Willie.

So we speeded up a bit, and there at last, a huge Liberal Arts Department sign appeared on the side of what looked an old tumbledown brick barn surrounded by motorbikes. We went up some rickety wooden stairs and into a large shabby room where about a dozen students were seated round a long table. They turned to look at us. I didn't know any of them. A tall guy at the end said,

"Come in. Glad you managed to find us. I've got you down as . . . yes, here it is . . . Trent and Williams. What do we call you?"

"Carl," said Willie, causing me to look at him in surprise. I'd forgotten. "Pete."

"Right, my name's Joe Greenaway, and I'm this group's personal tutor so we'll be seeing quite a lot of each other and I'm the guy you harass if you've got any difficulties, and I do hope you won't be afraid to do just that. This room is your home base while you're at the College, so you'll be spending some time here. I'm sorry that you've landed what is probably the oldest and shabbiest room in the entire place, but I'm not really because I happen to like it, so I only apologize to those who mind it."

Sitting down, I looked round and saw what he meant. The walls were battered beyond plastering, the wooden floor had gaps nearly wide enough to swallow Willie. An old stove stood black and dusty in the middle of a wall and drunken bookcases lurched on the others, covered in piles of books ancient and modern. But it was hung with pieces of writing, poems, drawings, paintings everywhere, a giant model of a building,

40

unfinished, stood in one corner of the room. And right in front of me was an enormous swirling picture filling the top of the wall. I looked at it and descended down and down and round into the centre of it as if it was music. Underneath was written The Waste Land.

I expected that after we'd nattered for a bit, and found out names, there'd be the usual page for us to write. I imagined we might have got a bit past What I Did in the Summer Holidays, but it would be after those lines. But no. We did natter, but about war, when or if it is ever justified, and then for something entertaining to finish off with he read us a poem called "Ping Pong" about table tennis, and showed us how the poet had played with the words like the game itself. This led on to more play with words, which I'd never thought about before and I wondered if my mucho aggro entered word play territory, though I didn't mention it.

As we walked home Willie said, "I like that. He's good."

"Yeh, OK for starters. I'll see how it is later when we have to get down to the nitty gritty."

"You sound like my Gran, boring Pete Twit," he grinned, and as I kicked him a few times and beat him about the ribs to show him his proper place, I remembered what the new room had reminded me of. My old one at home, safe and shabby and secure, before Dad and I had messed and mucked it about, making it clean and tidy and ruined for ever.

Verna was lording it in the coffee bar, and as we entered, she called us over.

"There will," she announced, "be a disco on Saturday. It's the Beginning of Term disco and we are all going to go. Especially you, Pete, you will be there and you will dance with me."

Claire grabbed my sweater to stop me from leaving the hut

rather faster than I'd come in. "I knew you'd cut and run," she said.

"I don't want to go. I don't like discos."

"How do you know? You've never been to one," said Judas Iscariot Willie Carl Trent.

"I just know. They'll be noisy and crowded and I shall get a headache and someone will be sick on me and someone else will pick a fight and some girl will think I insulted her when I haven't and slap my face and set her boy friend on to me . . ." I paused for breath.

"Caw. I didn't know you could say all that. I've only heard you manage one word at a time before this," Claire exclaimed.

Nick lounged across, followed by Oliver and Kenny.

"Pete, you're white with terror," grinned Oliver.

"The thought of dancing with Claire and Verna is enough to make anyone white with terror," said Nick and was stamped upon.

"It's settled. We're all going. No arguing, Pete."

"I'm not arguing. I'm not going, that's all."

"Will Sara be going?"

"What's that to do with you, Oliver?" said Willie, eyeing him up bitterly.

"I think it will be a really super evening. Let's get everyone we can to go," cried Verna.

"You lot can do what you like. I shall watch telly, as always."

"You coward, Pete Williams."

The word coward arose up in a nasty shape in the night and mocked me from the bottom of the bed. Mucho aggro, huh. Pete Williams runs and hides away. Cowardy, cowardy custard. Thought you'd decided to change, but you're still wet and feeble just like a drippy girl. That's a laugh! What's wet

42

about the girls you know? Sal and Verna and Claire are like terrible Amazons.

And I remembered the face I'd seen that first morning, the funny, worried face belonging to someone who didn't look in the least like Sal and Verna and Claire, but little and lost and not coping very well. Smaller than me, making me feel nine foot high and brave as a lion . . . disco . . . coward . . . I was starting to feel sleepy again . . . wonder if she'll go . . . I . . . hadn't . . . seen her . . . at the College since but she was there . . . that morning . . . she might go to the disco . . . if so, I'll go . . . .

"You're an angel," said Verna. But I knew you'd come if I asked you, darling Peterkin."

Various guys looked at me enviously, he's doing all right, what on earth's he got written all over them.

4

On Saturday morning I lay in bed till I heard Dad enquiring loudly whether the indolent, useless layabout that he'd had the dubious honour of fathering was thinking of taking to his bed permanently, and if so would he be required to take his meals up and generally w˃it on him. This speech rumbled on for some time, so I had a chance to get dressed before he flung open the door and said had I remembered I was supposed to be helping Sal move some gear today and had I also thought of moving out?

"Then all the little chicks will be flown from the nest," he beamed, looking like Orson Welles in one of those old films. "Goody."

I'd forgotten Sal was going and I rushed downstairs feeling guilty, but various friends of hers had turned up with an old van, and she drove off, saying she'd see me that evening at the disco.

"Disco?"

"I'm going to one. I think," sudden doubts sweeping over me.

"You don't mean to say you're going out? Leaving the house? On a Saturday? Boy, you astonish me. I thought you were a permanent fixture in the evening, seated before the telly with your mother and myself. I'm not sure how I shall survive without you. Match of the Day just won't be the same. We've watched it for years together."

"Do stop tormenting him, Colin. I'm very pleased he's

going out with his friends. Are they the ones coming down the street? There seems to be a whole gang of them.''

I looked and there was a whole gang of them, Nick, Willie, Oliver, Kenny, Verna and Claire and a couple of others. They bore down on our house.

"What a horrible-looking bunch," Dad was saying. "Can they be for real? Is that the cream of today's youth coming here? I'd pull up the drawbridge and man the barricades if we'd got any. As it is I think I'll hide in a cupboard somewhere. I don't feel strong enough to encounter them.''

Verna, ahead of the others, smiled at him and he paused for a moment.

"That one can come again. The others have a three-month ban after today. Let them know," and he disappeared. But Ma welcomed them all in smiling, rustling up coffee. The house was full.

"I remember them now," said Verna. "Your Dad's dishy. And your mother's nice." I thought so, too, then I saw she'd captured Kenny and was talking to him in the careful, lip-shaping way she uses with her slow learners. Ma had found more material. He was watching her as if hypnotized.

"He'd better look out. Ma teaches literacy at the prison in her spare time.''

"That'll be handy," Oliver said. "He can keep on with his course if he gets nicked.''

"Is that supposed to be funny?" asked Claire.

Ma was saying, "Tell me, Kenny. Have you got any problems?" Kenny made one of his usual grunts, but she must've picked up something.

"No, you poor thing. Really, it must be so hard for you. Look, be sure and come to me if you get in any difficulties. You know where I live now and I'll give you the phone number before you go. We'll see what we can do.''

"It's Oliver what's got de real troubles," said Kenny.

45

"He's been thrown out by his ole man."

"Oh, no," cried Ma. "Why did he throw you out?"

"He said he couldn't stand me any longer, gave me fifty quid and showed me the door," Oliver explained calmly.

"Sensible fellow, your father," said mine, putting in a brief appearance searching for his pipe.

Ma had gone white. "How wicked. How unspeakably wicked to do that to you. How could anyone do that to their own child . . . ?"

"Very easily, I imagine," put in Dad, pocketing his pipe, smiling at Verna and going out again.

"What are you going to do? Where will you sleep? Have you got enough money to live on?" Ma was off, rattling like a machine gun now. "You can always stay here. We've got plenty of room. Sometimes I feel guilty about it when everywhere people are enduring such hardship. All those problems. Of course you can come here. Especially now Sara's going. And, of course, Peter can always double up."

"Hey," I cried in protest at the mind-boggling thought of doubling up with Oliver or Kenny.

"Actually, I'm fine," smiled Oliver. "I've got a room at Kenny's house and his Mum's looking after me."

"My Mum likes 'm."

"As long as you're all right."

"I think he'd be all right anywhere, like an alley cat," Claire said, getting up. "And now we're off."

"We came to make sure you'd turn up tonight," added Verna, wrinkling her nose at me. We drifted to the door, Ma still talking earnestly to Oliver, who was smiling, there's something someone said about smiling, I can't remember what.

"The last thing you want in this house is that pair," whispered Claire in my ear.

"Why?" I hissed back. "I mean, I don't anyway, but what's the reason?"

46

"I'll tell you some time."

"Are you all going then?" cried Dad, emerging. "Jolly good. Don't let me keep you. Oh, no, look who's coming, now. I'm off to the Ring o' Bells if she's dropping in."

It was Aunt Sybil, ignoring me, flinching at the sight of Claire, Verna and Willie, and pausing to speak to Oliver and Nick. I wondered why till I heard, "Of course I know your mothers . . ."

"You coming?" asked Claire, irritably.

"Dunno."

"Make up your mind."

I could hear Aunt Sybil saying to Ma, "Colin's always in a hurry when he sees me. Still, I'm glad Peter has found two nice friends at last. I know their mothers. The smaller one's mother's a very good bridge player."

That decided me.

"I'm coming with you, Claire. Hang on."

By six that evening I was full of doubts. I didn't want to go to a disco. And that didn't mean I was a coward I told myself. It showed I'd got some sense. It would be boring, and I'd be sure to fall over my own feet and make a fool of myself. I always did, and a disco wouldn't be any different. Besides, I didn't feel too good. That wasn't a let-out, I definitely had the beginnings of a sore throat. I really wasn't fit enough to go. I probably had a cold coming. I'd tell them when they arrived to pick me up that I'd developed this sore throat — which was getting worse all the time now I'd thought about it — and it wouldn't be fair to go with them in case they all got it. I can't stand people who go around giving their colds and sore throats to everybody, it's most unfair. Probably if I stayed in quietly watching telly and having an early night it would go away and I'd be perfectly all right by tomorrow. I know that sounded a bit as if I'd settled for very early retirement but it wasn't like that really, it was just, well . . .

The girl. What about the girl? Suppose she went and I missed her. She might dance with Nick, yuck, Willie, yuck, Oliver, double yuck, Kenny, no, nobody would dance with Kenny. But she wouldn't go to a disco. She didn't look the kind of girl who'd do things like going to discos. No, she'd be helping the aged or studying quietly and getting it slightly wrong, perhaps going for a walk with her mother (stone the crows, we'll make a dazzling pair, me with early retirement and her helping the aged . . .)

At that point Willie arrived with Claire and Verna, Claire's hair a new and extraordinary colour like blue beetroot, Verna's an extraordinary colour anyway, but by nature.

"Come on," the girls said, taking my arms.

"I don't think I'm coming," I squeaked, at least that's how it sounded.

"Don't bother to argue," Claire said.

"Darling Peterkin," Verna said.

"I had nothing to do with it," cried Willie, hopping along beside us for they were moving me at great speed. "Sorry."

"The others are coming later. I think they're hoping to go to a pub first. Oliver's eighteen, you see, and the others are big so they'll probably be all right."

"Not fair," muttered Willie, for although he's six foot two no one would ever take him to be older than he is, sixteen.

"Can we slow down? I'm out of breath. And where is this place?"

"Quite a way yet."

It was. In one of the far outposts of the College, in one of their many buildings, but we got there at last.

It was horrible, as I thought it would be. I've never liked disco and the disc jockey was playing a terrible selection much too

48

loud even for me and I like loud music. I had a shandy and wished I hadn't as Claire then seized me and made me bounce all round the room like a maniac, and every time I stopped she seized me and wound me up once more, and the coloured lights and the horrible noise and the heat of the bodies and the smell mixed with the shandy fizzing up and down me, for I really did feel ill, now, and I wished I wasn't there. If this was fun, then give me straight torture. Verna seized me next and pounded me back and forth a bit while the sweat poured off me. I didn't ask if anyone else was enjoying themselves as I wouldn't have heard the answer, besides they wouldn't have heard the question. Suddenly a vast hand grabbed Verna and hauled her away. She squawked desperately at me, but I crept away to sit in the merciful quiet of a particularly dark corner and recover.

Slowly I came to and after a bit crept off to buy myself another shandy and retreat to the safety of my corner once more and look around to see if by any chance the girl had turned up, though I didn't think it likely. I watched the room as the spotlight turned on different dancers, changing them into kaleidoscopic colours. It seized on Claire, who looked amazing, turning and moving in her tiny skirt combined with wellies and a shiny top with no straps. In the cloakroom she'd fixed two boppers with butterflies on them to her head. Then the spotlight settled on Verna, changing to all gold, and I had to admit, very pretty, and on her partner, Kenny, so that was who the huge mauler belonged to was it? Actually he moved very lightly, I saw with a sinking of the heart, he'd be nippy in a scrap, not that I ever wanted to be in a fight with him, for I should just be an all time loser.

I tried to peer into the further corners of the room to see if I could see the girl but they were too dark, so very daringly I made a circuit, peering at people, taking care to avoid my crowd, and then sat down again, for she wasn't there, although a great many other people were. I looked at my watch,

squinting hard to see what the time was for by now I was so
bored and wishing I was at home, and I wanted to know how
many hours I'd still got to endure as I supposed we'd have to
stay till the bitter end. I wondered what was on telly, and then
the music changed, moving into one of my records I liked. And
it was magic. The lights softened, changed their rhythm along
with the altered beat of the music, and I was lost, gone in my
own world, my dream world, out, over and beyond. I closed
my eyes and the room vanished. I had forgotten everything,
forgotten that this was the other side of the coin.

It was a long time later. Someone was shaking me. I opened
my eyes and it was Verna, and the others behind her.

"He's gone, really gone," she was saying. "Pete, are you all
right? Open your eyes. Come on. Hey, you're not drunk, are
you? Idiot."

"Of course I'm not. I only had two shandies. And anyone
who grew up with my ole man can surely drink two shandies.
Hey, it's gone quiet."

"It's the interval. Come on, we're going to get some
snacks."

I didn't want to bother for there was a large crowd, but she
hauled me behind her. I pulled back a bit, and a big bloke who
really did look as if he'd had too much suddenly grabbed Oliver
just beside me and snarled, "Who d'you think you're pushing
around?" He had a mate with him.

I opened my mouth to speak, for the pair looked like trouble,
nasty trouble, but Oliver just flicked his fingers and there, out
of the blue, was Kenny.

"You want to make something of it?" Oliver asked, gently.

"Yeah," began one, but the other pulled at him.

"No, no. Sorry," he said. "Forget it. I didn't see it was
you." And melted away, the other following.

And that little episode stayed with me long after I was in bed,
the music still ringing in my ears, having enjoyed the second

half better, assuring the girls I'd had a smashing time, danced a bit more, seen Willie turn green with jealousy at the sight of Sal with a new boy friend who wore a suit! Something wrong with him, said Willie.

And I fell asleep, thinking no girl there, and remembering I didn't see it was you. Strange, very strange.

5

"You lot have nearly become the 'in' scene," Sal grinned. "For what it's worth."

She'd dropped in to collect some more stuff for her flat and was drinking coffee with Willie, Nick, Verna and me. We'd come home for lunch since the queues were so long, and it was always our house people came to as it was the nearest to College and the nearest to the town centre.

"That's Verna. She's so flash everyone notices her."

"Hark who's talking. You're the show-off round here, Nick."

"Seriously, you two could probably become the first year representatives on the committee if you're interested," Sal said. "How about it? We need some lively new blood. Last year's lot, between ourselves, are as dead as dodos."

"I wouldn't mind, actually," said Verna.

"With my tremendous charm and charisma, I should get in easily," drawled Nick.

"That's enough to make me stand against you . . ."

"I must fly," sighed Sal, looking at her watch. "Think about it. And you, Pete."

"Not me, I'm the unpolitical member of the family."

"You always get things wrong, Pete. The Students' Union isn't about politics."

"What is it about then?"

"Mostly students' welfare. And organization . . ." she got

52

up. "I must fly. I've got a meeting of the Academic Board . . ."

"Sounds grand."

"It's usually pretty tedious and boring. Cheerio."

"Can I come along with you?" asked Willie eagerly.

"What, to the meeting?"

"No, along the road."

"No, Tony's giving me a lift. Bye."

"Better luck next time," said Nick.

"It's no good, you can't compete with this Tony guy, he's studying law at the University and is posh," I said, thinking the sooner Willie got the situation clear the better.

"Better settle for Claire. She fancies you," said Verna wickedly.

Willie looked as if he didn't want to settle for Claire and the door bell rang, as it does a lot these days, so that Dad speaks about barricades, bans and pouring boiling oil from the parapets. Verna let in Oliver and Kenny.

"Coming to the amusement arcade, Pete?" asked Oliver.

"No, I've got to get back."

"What the hell for? It's a nice afternoon. Don't waste your time at that old dump. Come with us. See life. And you three. Come on."

"No, I've got to go. I've got Joe this afternoon."

"So what? Afternoon sessions are a complete waste of time, you always fall asleep, especially if you've had a pint at lunch time. Come on."

Kenny stood over me, reeking like a brewery. "Come on, Pete, you come, even if the others are chicken." I stepped sideways and so did he. No one felt more chicken than me as I thought for one wild moment he was going to cart me off bodily, and the last thing I wanted to do at that moment was to go to the amusement arcade with them. And Sal rushed in.

"I forgot my folder. Hey, you're a bit late, aren't you all?"

"Yes, we must go."

"I can give some of you a lift. Pile in with Tony. He won't mind. I don't think we can manage you two, though." That was to Kenny and Oliver.

Oliver smiled at her. "That's OK. We're going in another direction, anyway, Sara."

For a minute they stared at one another.

"Yes, I imagine we are," she said, then, "Here, get in the rest of you. It'll be a bit of a squash. Meet Tony. Tony, my brother and his pals."

Willie sat at the back, eyes crossing with hatred, staring at Tony's neck, covered with fair curling hair.

Joe was getting me to write a bit, not a lot, but something. For ages I could only manage about three words though I used to cover pages and pages at the Primary school. But at Rolleston Boys, after I wrote about a fight and all the aggro words were crossed out with don't use such language in your school work, I lost interest. We were reading *Kes* at the time and the comment on my story didn't seem to make much sense, but then, I'd given up expecting school to make much sense.

Joe was playing music, Bach, Bartok and Bowie. It was great but I was afraid that it would be ruined by having to write such turgid rot as I find this piece of music very interesting at the end of it. For that is where I'd arrive at the barrier and come to a halt, but it was OK, fine, all he asked us to do was to write down any words that matched the music. So I listened and jotted down words, and they wove together moving in and out, under and over, back and through, and when I'd finished I watched the Waste Land collapsing and decaying and melting into swirling patterns sifting and drifting down into my mind.

Nick was having a birthday party and we were all invited, including Sal and Tony.

"Is there no end to your mad social whirl? This feverish

round of wild delight?" asked my father. "I find it astonishing. I hope you're not intending to give one here. The thought of your giant-hoofed friends tripping the light fantastic to your hellish music would be too much for my delicate constitution let alone the house."

"I think he's only having a few friends in," I replied, but it turned out to be a large party when we got there. I wondered if he was taking Sal's ideas seriously and trying to catch the votes as there were so many students. Nick's parents are rich, very, his Dad makes buckets or dustbins or something and there were appropriately buckets of food and drink, and a huge bowl of punch. The house was large and two rooms had had the partitions pulled back and the furniture cleared. I stood behind something trailing and hideous which turned out to be plastic vine leaves. I had hoped to lurk there for some time but was hauled out to leap about with Verna, then Claire, and to my extreme horror Sal, who meanly said that as I seemed to be taking up dancing at last then I could do so with her as well. I trod on her feet for revenge and she limped off saying that that was the first and last with me.

I saw her again quite soon. Nick picked her out with a spotlight standing alone in the middle of the room. A really hypnotic number started to play and Sal began to dance on her own. She swayed there in the centre of the floor while the colours changed from turquoise to green and then yellow and orange into a golden rose, Sal still swaying in the middle until she was joined by a figure keeping just out of the light — a thin figure in black, who kept time and step with Sal, while everyone watched. Then the guy reached forward, took Sal's hands and pulled her towards him, and as he did so Claire leapt into the dance, with her great wellie jump, everyone joined in and in no time there was a heap of bodies bouncing about.

When at last the lights went up I saw that it was Oliver who had been dancing with Sal.

The noise and the flashing coloured lights had given me a headache so I wandered into the kitchen where the grub was and sat down by the punch, which was great. I had another glass and another. Nick was on top form, organizing everything and putting himself about generally. After a time, he filled my glass up with something else, his Dad's whisky, single malt, fantastic, don't tell anyone, Dad'll go spare he hissed at me, then disappeared to jive with Claire, a nasty sight that made me feel giddy, so I had some lager to clear it, my head, I mean, and was then joined by Verna who sat on my knee, and removed my glasses, which always makes me agitated, but she calmed me down and I found that after a while she was nursing me, and from what I could see Claire was nursing Willie. It was necessary to go to the bog, so I wandered upstairs and got lost among the many bodies engaged in all sorts of things I'd only read about in books and seen on telly. Somebody seized me and cried, "Here's a nice little spare one," but another voice said, "Watch it, that's Sara Williams's brother."

"No, I'm not," I found I was saying with great dignity. "I don't know the girl at all. And I don't like her. She treads on people."

I felt proud of this, and about the way I got downstairs again. It was just a case of concentrating hard, I decided.

Someone shouted, "That's my head you're standing on," but I took no notice. I was anxious to get back to my seat beside the punch, a good place to be. Kenny and Nick came, I could see it was them quite clearly, they were rubbing their hands and looking pleased with themselves.

"We've just thrown out two second years who were looking for trouble," Nick said triumphantly. "Pity you missed it, Pete. Big guys they were too. Yes, you should've been there."

"Ug," Kenny said, a long speech for him.

I nodded up and down. "Yes, wish I'd been there," and stopped nodding for my head didn't seem to be going up and down in the usual way. From somewhere a girl had appeared and was kissing me. That was all right, but I suddenly remembered THE GIRL. Suppose she was here and saw me kissing this one — who was it? — oh, yes, a girl in my Maths group, marvellous at logarithms they said, didn't need to use the tables, what was I doing kissing a girl like that? I didn't want to be unfaithful to my dream girl with a logarithm table! Not even a walking, talking, kissing one. I stood up.

"I've got to look for the girl," I said to Willie, who seemed to be sitting on the floor.

"There are dozens of girls here. You don't need to look for one," said Nick. "You've got the two prettiest anyway, Sal and Verna, amazing."

"I don't like them much. Treaders and tramplers." It's hard to say treaders and tramplers so it came out as shedders and shamplers.

And I was walking home between Sal and Tony, and each time I took a step I sank forward on to my knees before rising up again so that it was slow. Someone behind us was singing, and Tony was telling them to shut up else we'd all be arrested. I grew interested in the strange, swinging paths the stars were making across the skies, and I pointed them out to Sal but she didn't think much of them.

"Where's Willie? I want Willie. Willie would like to shee the shtarss danshing. Willie likesh thatsh short of thing."

"Don't disturb him. He's behind with Oliver and Kenny and they're concentrating on their feet."

There were some nasty noises behind us as well.

"There goes poor Willie," said Sal.

"Shilly Billy Willie. Shouldn't get drunk. Should shjust get happy like me. I am sherry happy."

"That makes a change," Sal said from several miles away and

57

we had to wait for her to get herself back again, shilly girl. "Normally, you're dead miserable."

"Acksherly, I've been happy for shome time now."

This idea came as such a shock to me that I sat down in the road and decided to stay there for it was so comfortable. But Sal was cruel and made me get up again. Nashty Sal, Nashty Shal, you've been nashty all evening.

"You may be happy now but just wait till morning," she said right in my ear, ever sho loudly, just how mean can you be?

"Thash my house. I can get up the shteps myself." As I was managing nicely on my hands and knees Shal said,

"Whatever will Ma say? Pete's never been . . ."

The docr opened. I floated in on air, like a bird, like a bird, and fell flat on my face at Dad's feet.

"It must be Christmas," he said as I struggled to my feet, "and this is a little gift for us." I waved him aside in a lordly manner and all the people behind fell back down the steps. I had to speak with my mother.

"Ma," I said, waving my arm once more.

"Look out back there," Dad called out, but from the noise it was too late.

"Ma, Bedzz, they all need bedzz," I said.

"What, all of them?"

"Ma, it's all right, really." Nashty Shall interfering again. Shan't Shall.

"Shut up, Shall. They need bedzzz. They can't walk home."

"Fancy," my father said. "I'd never have guessed. Did you have a good drink, then, Pete, lad? Good lad. You'll feel terrible tomorrow."

"Don't forget, Ma. Bedzzzz." I tried to make the stairs but they shouldn't put shstairs sho far away, far away, and shuch a shilly shape, going upsh and downs in and out like shthat. I remembered shomeshing.

"Dad, look after Willie. Shilly Willie hash drunksh too much."

And just then I had a thought. If I lay down on the shtairs for the night there'd be a bedzz for someone else so I lay . . . down
. . .

"Here we go," said Dad, as I was heaved up like a sack of potatoes. And there I went.

6

"The body is a lousy, rotten handicap. It needs feeding. It needs bathing. It needs shaving. And it gets nagovers, I mean hangovers, no, I was right the first time. Ooh, ooh, ooh. Sal, why are you stamping? Why are you so unkind to me?"

I was lying fully dressed on my bed while Sal did a clog dance round the room. There'd been a sandstorm in my mouth in the night, and the grains of sand were still there, the storm having exposed a local sewage farm from the feel and taste of it. Someone was banging moderately heavily on my head with a giant crowbar. He had a good beat.

Sal loomed over me. "I've brought you some coffee. And an aspirin."

"I can't sit up."

"Yes, you can. Here, I'll help."

"Why are you shouting?"

"I'm not. I'm whispering. That's right. Drink it all. Get your sweater off and get under the clothes and I'll wake you again later."

I fell asleep before she'd stamped out of the room.

Later I got up and went very slowly downstairs. Ma was feeding what looked like Polyfilla to Kenny and making clucking noises, assuring him that this was an old Northern cure for a hangover. Oliver was drinking black coffee, looking like the before part of a before and after ad. Yuck, I thought, and went in search of Willie, finding him asleep with bits of him curled and wedged into a wardrobe, head on shoes. Together we went downstairs, shaky but coping.

"Vitamin C," said Sal handing us orange juice. "Essential."

"Do you have to be so bright and healthy?"

"I kept away from that punch. Heaven knows what had gone into it."

"Why aren't you at the flat?"

"I stayed to help Ma. And Dad's taken Tony for a drink . . ."

". . . don't mention that word . . ."

"And we're staying for Sunday lunch."

In the end Willie stayed as well, as he wanted to be quite recovered when he saw his Gran or she'd worry. Dad on returning said he could possibly stand Willie as he'd known him for too many years, but the others must go or receive a life ban. They went.

"I don't feel much like eating," said Willie as we sat down.

"Rubbish. It will make you feel much better," Dad announced firmly, and I did feel better after some soup, and then Ma came in with the roast. She hates cooking.

"We don't eat meat at home," announced Willie sadly.

"How sensible," Ma cried. "I'm thinking of becoming a vegetarian."

Dad, who loves roast, glared a bit, but carried on eating. The meat was very tough.

"I think that if we didn't eat meat there'd be more food for everyone because of the amount cows eat. Humans haven't got the teeth for meat-eating."

"This would give piranha fish trouble," growled Dad, masticating vigorously. Willie spoke on.

"I think it would be a good step forward if the human race gave up eating meat . . ."

I'd been waiting for Dad to crack and he did.

"Why don't you shut up so that we can carry on the struggle

in peace?'' he bellowed, putting down his knife and fork.

Ma laid hers down as well. ''The life of a woman is so frustrating and thankless that some appreciation is needed to make it even fractionally worth while . . .''

''Women! Women! I've nothing against women. I quite fancy them at times, though less and less as the years take their toll. No, they're perfectly all right . . . except that they're useless . . . useless . . . though, mind you, not so useless as him . . .''

I knew it would get back to me.

''Why do you always discourage him? It's bad for him.''

I looked at Tony, watching in fascination, mouth open, fork paused with a bit of meat on it. Willie groaned to himself. I think he felt too ill to care. Sal went on eating.

''I'm not wasting this. I don't think I've eaten all week,'' she said to herself.

''Bad for him! It's me he's bad for. He's been bad for me for years now. Why doesn't he get a job and go away? Somewhere. Anywhere. Please.''

A despairing vision of the future unfolded before me.

''I don't suppose I shall ever get a job. I can't imagine me having a job.''

''Neither can I,'' groaned my father. ''Yet, why not? Why not even you? There must be something you can do. I tell you what, I'll help you.''

''No thanks. When the time comes, I'll fail to get my own job, thank you very much.''

''Jolly good,'' Sal cried.

We struggled on with the meal but it was proving too much.

''This is bigger than I am. I give up,'' Dad said, laying down his knife and fork. We all did.

''I hate waste,'' Ma said sadly. ''There's enough food here to keep a family in the third world for a week.''

There's not a lot you can say to that but Dad managed.

"Pack it up in a parcel then and send it there by first class mail."

But Ma soon rallied, directed us into doing the washing up, gave us some notices to deliver and then went upstairs to do some more work on reading problems, though not before she'd tried one of her Home Grown Instant Intelligence Tests on Tony. Sal told me she'd already warned him about this so he seemed to be coping. We sat reading the Sundays waiting for him, Willie groaning at intervals, he said he still felt ill, when Dad bore down on Sal rather like one of the latest tanks bearing down on a bombarded city.

"That one is a nerd. Of the lowest order of nerds," he hissed out of the side of his mouth. I agreed with him but Sal looked hurt.

"What d'you mean? I thought you liked him."

"Can't stand him. A creep, that's what he is. You can't have him. He'll have to go."

"How can you say that? You've only just met him. And look how handsome he looks talking to Ma."

"Anyone would look handsome talking to your mother. It's the contrast. No, he won't do. Get rid of him. There's no bottle to him."

"What do you mean there's no bottle?" They were both hissing angrily at each other now.

"Bottle, guts, stomach."

"Thank goodness he hasn't got any, then. He doesn't want all that at his age!"

"I mean I wouldn't go into the jungle with him."

"But the last thing I want to do is go into the jungle with him. Or anyone else for that matter. You are a silly old fool, Dad."

Tony came over then and they shut up.

I don't think Tony and Sal wanted us with 'em much, not

surprising, but we promised we'd leave 'em alone when we got there, at least I did, but the whole thing was really Willie's idea, because he was so jealous of Tony that he didn't want them driving off on their own. None of this appealed to me much but I didn't mind an outing as I thought some fresh air might blow my head clear. So we drove through the lanes with autumn leaves flinging themselves everywhere to the Tower built by some maniac years ago. We used to go there when Sal and I were little, and for some reason she wanted to show it to Tony as it was a part of her she wanted him to know. I had the feeling that this kind of conversation was a complete waste of time with dear Tony and I was right. She'd have done better telling Willie about Childhood Days at the Tower.

"It's pathetic," Tony said, getting out of the car, "half falling down and a sham into the bargain. I bet it's full of junk. Why couldn't we have gone to Castle . . . ?" and he named the famous one round here that every tourist visits. "That should have been worth seeing."

Sal was pink. "But I like it because it's tatty . . . like Mervyn Peake's old and crumbling parapet . . ."

That meant nothing to me and I could see it meant nothing to Tony either. Sal's eyes looked watery. "Watch it, she'll either burst into tears or hit you where it hurts, mate," I thought, and hoped for the second.

"Sorry, but I don't like the shoddy and second rate," he said, smiling with perfect teeth, a very good-looking guy if you like those models in shop windows.

"Oh."

"Don't worry about it. I can always find something to interest me wherever I go. Come on, then." You could nearly hear the let's get it over with in his voice. I looked at Willie to see what he was going to do and he'd put himself on the other side of Sal.

"I think it's a beautiful tower, Sal, especially with all the trees and the battlements and everything."

Tony looked at him as if he was some alien and inferior form of life, and I moved away, for I wanted to go up on the top where the view's terrific and sniff the air by myself, for other people's problems get very tedious if you get too much of them, nearly as bad as your own. I ran quickly up the spiral staircase, then regretted it as it brought on the dizzies again, and looked over the parapet at the view. Which is absolutely splattering, miles and miles and miles of it but it wasn't that that caused my hair to stand up on end, ears to roar, teeth to chatter, and the trembles take me over. No. There on the smoothish grass at the bottom of the Tower, with the path coming up from the valley, there with sheep and the couple of old benches, there, she was. I looked and looked. I couldn't move. I could only tremble. She wore a floaty sort of dress and her hair was tangly. A shaft of autumn sunlight caught her there and she looked like a cobweb, not for real. She started to walk away and I woke up.

"Hey, wait, wait for me," I cried. "Hey." But she was already moving away towards the path. There was an instant when I thought about jumping over the parapet and landing at her feet, the Sixth Form College's answer to Tarzan. Then I ran for the steps and hurtled down them as fast as I could go, missing steps, leaping across landings. I must get to her. I reached the bottom floor, crammed with statues, pictures, monuments, awful furniture, agricultural implements, and the two old boys who own the Tower selling tenpenny tickets. They stood blocking my way out, and they were arguing with Tony.

"You didn't pay," said the sandy one.

"You mustn't sneak in without paying," said the toothy one.

"Excuse me," I shouted, going insane.

No one took any notice, they just stood there, the two old men, Tony, Sal and Willie, and wouldn't budge an inch.

"Please let me pass!"

"I didn't sneak in without paying."

"You must have done because you haven't got a ticket, have you?"

"Let me through. Willie! Move!"

"There wasn't anybody here to get a ticket from," said Tony.

"That's your story."

"It's not a story."

"Fellow's a scoundrel, Humphrey."

"Not the thing, Jeffrey."

They moved at last and as I tore down the path I could hear cries of "The youth of today, Jeffrey!" "Absolutely deplorable, Humphrey!" and then I was running like a Seb Coe clone.

But she'd completely disappeared of course.

I searched and searched but it was no good. There wasn't a trace of her. I sat moodily under a tree for some time, then decided I'd better see what had happened to the others. I couldn't find them either until I came upon Tony and Sal having a snog by an old stone bridge. They didn't see me but I saw Willie, who was leaning miserably on a gate near by .

"Willie," I whispered, at least I thought it was a whisper, but Tony must have ears like a bat picking up radar. He looked up, and his face mottled unprettily. Mottle was not his colour.

"You sneaky little pair of voyeurs," he shouted, and then turned to Sal. "I'm going home. And if the rest of you want a lift back you'd better come now, or else walk."

Off he strode at enormous speed, us trotting behind saying sorry from time to time, then we drove home in a cold and nasty silence. I stared out of the window, full of gloom and disappointment, and when I saw Kenny and Oliver sitting on the pavement with several guys, who looked the roughest and toughest bunch of weirdos I'd ever seen in this town, I couldn't raise the energy to mention it. They were all passing round something.

What I know about the drug scene could be written on the back of a halfpenny, but it looked as if they were passing round a joint. Not in daylight, in the street, surely. I pushed it out of my mind.

In any case I'd got three pieces of work to get ready for Monday morning. But when I'd done them I could put on a record, lie on my bed and think about how she'd looked that afternoon at the Tower.

7

Work wasn't going too badly. Yes, there was the time I blew up something in the chemistry lab, and the time I upset Indian ink all over Joe's final scripts for the magazine we were producing, and the time when I set fire to the waste bin in the coffee bar, but all in all it could've been worse. I hadn't had to mutter my mantra much and the evening of the trench was far away. Perhaps the work wasn't too difficult because I'd done some of it before, and I didn't mind the lecturers, but mainly I wasn't so uptight and harassed by the knife-edged competition there'd been at Rolleston Boys. Or maybe it was because we worked in smaller groups, or because I wasn't supposed to be working for the honour of the school or the house.

Most probably it was because the girls were there. Verna and Claire both helped me, Claire especially was brilliant. She intended getting to Cambridge to do Pure Maths, chewing gum, stripy hair, football socks and all.

"You were going to tell me about Oliver," I said to her one day in the library where we'd finished some Physics — Physics will baffle me to the end of my days — and were sitting in a quiet little alcove.

"Yeh, yeh," she said, taking out some more gum. She looked around to check that we were on our own.

"I know a few things about him, because my Mum used to be their cleaning lady. They're filthy rich, the Olivers . . ."

"Olivers? But that's his Christian name."

"Yes, it is. He's called Oliver Oliver. All the eldest sons are."

"Yuck."

"I know. I think he probably thinks so, too, for he never mentions it. Anyway when I was little I used to go with my Mum up to their house in the school holidays so I've known him for ages. He's got a younger brother and sister and they're all right if you like huntin' and shootin' that is. Their house is really beautiful, not like Nick's with all those plastic gadgets, but old and, well, just beautiful. Anyway, he always tried to get me into trouble from the first . . . like breaking something, then saying it was me. Once he stole some money and I got the blame, then there was a helluva stink and I didn't go again, stayed with my Gran instead even when they found out later he'd nicked it. But he was a horrible little kid, the sort who pulls wings off flies. Once he cut the whiskers off the cat, no, it's not funny, they can't walk properly because it upsets their balance . . . he must have been the complete opposite of you, Pete . . ."

"I was pretty horrible, as well. Ask Sal."

"Verna says you were sweet, but you had a terrible temper and used to kiss her behind the holly bush."

"Shut up. Go on about Oliver."

"You're blushing."

"Pack it in, will you? You see I saw him with a really hard-looking crowd, death in the afternoon, and they seemed to be smoking a joint sitting on the pavement."

"Nothing would surprise me about that lot. Or him. My Mum went back to work at their house again, after they'd offered her extra money — she's a good worker, you see — so I still heard about him from time to time."

"Such as?"

"Well, for a start, he was expelled from three schools, mostly for stealing, but there was something else about the

69

third, a bit nasty, I don't know what, and some kid committed suicide. So they sent him to Nick's, where he settled down, and since he's bright enough, got ten or eleven O Levels, but even so, he's still been in trouble with the police in the holidays and he's on probation, or has been. I do know the fuzz still keep their eye on him, his mother's had a nervous breakdown and his father's thrown him out . . ."

"And he lives with Kenny. What about Kenny?"

"Oh, he's just a thickie, a no-hoper. But he's a hard man and Oliver uses him. He'll drop out of college any time now, I should think."

"What about that crowd I saw them with?"

"That's probably Pat Rieber's gang, which means he's out again, pity. Was there an ash-blond bloke there?"

"Yeah, nasty."

"That's Zed Clements. He's really unstable, a psychopath probably."

"How do you know all this?"

"My brother got mixed up with 'em, and the fuzz came round, but my Dad gave him such a belting he packed it all in and went to join the Navy. Establishment figure now. But he said I was never to go near 'em. They're really bent, and nasty with it. If Oliver's mixed up with them he's in dead trouble. And Pete . . ."

"Yeh?"

"Don't ever let Pat's lot near your house. And I'd tell your mother not to welcome Oliver and Kenny with quite such enthusiasm, because you can't trust them an inch."

"Ma's very tough."

"She may be. But different worlds y'know . . ."

"There you are. I wondered where you'd got to. Sneaking away with Peterkin, are you? Don't forget he's mine."

Verna planted a kiss on my left eyebrow, and my specs fell off. In the scuffle and giggling, a dragon appeared and slagged us all off for making a noise in an area which was supposed to be quiet.

I still looked for the girl. Every day. At least I knew she existed. I'd cycled up to the Tower a couple of times but there'd been no sign of her, and it was now closed to the public for the winter, and I didn't have the nerve to go up to the one old boy I saw there, who appeared to be gathering wood, looking like something out of Grimm's fairy tales.

I sat in the Waste Land room, hammering out a poem for this magazine we were producing.

> Peter Moonfool
> Is my friend
> I see him in the mirror
> He'll get me in the end.
>
> Every day I dress this way
> for my parents' sake.
> It's the way
> They say
>
> Peter Moonfool waits for me
> And soon some day
> I'll be free
> Peter's friend.
>
> And he'll have got me
> in the end.
> I'll be him
> and he'll
> be me.

I settled back in the chair and it happened.

A short, powerful, bald man in hairy tweeds walked in and started to talk very earnestly to Joe. His eyes — slitted behind his glasses, don't remind me — ran over the group who'd fallen silent but a-twitch to know what was going on, all except me praying for oblivion. I didn't want to know, I knew it was no good, I knew this would be nasty, it had all the hall-marks of being very nasty indeed.

He was carrying a sheaf of papers, no, they couldn't be, could they, not here, not where everything had seemed reasonable, all right, OK. At least up till now. The Weevil Bird with papers. Tests. They were bound to be tests. The Weevil Bird was a snake in the grass. The Weevil Bird was the serpent in Paradise, well, no, the Sixth Form College wasn't that good, but tests, really. They couldn't be doing reading ages. We ought to be past those by now. All my life I've done reading tests, all of them mad. Some had instructions so complicated you had to be genius-level to follow them in the first place, and back at Rolleston we did one where it didn't test the reading but how fast you could write in the silly provided slots, and my friend Paddy, who was reading *War and Peace* at the time, wouldn't write anything down and was sent back to the Remedial Class, where he sent the teacher spare.

Or maybe it would be the petrol pumps again. Spot the difference. As far as I could see there weren't any and if there were I didn't care. Petrol pumps are very boring and don't get less so for being drawn on paper with differences. Surely there are better things in life. But the Weevil Bird had the look of a petrol pump man. We were for it.

Joe was frowning.

"Not up to me. They're asking for a new assessment."

Joe shrugged his shoulders.

We were moved from round the table and spaced out, surprise,

surprise. And so it began. Some people, the test-lovers, were smiling.

"Put your names at the top," Joe intoned.

I sat there. I wanted to stand up and cry crap, but I didn't. No hero, me. You won't find me at the barricades.

But I didn't write anything at all on the paper, except my name.

"Sucks to tests and weevil birds," I thought as I handed it in.

I wandered off on my own, didn't feel like talking to anyone. I mooched around, hoping to see the girl. She might walk round the corner, just like that and smile at me, and I'd say casually,

"Coming for a coffee?" and she'd say,

"That'd be terrific," and we'd walk away together. Life being what it is I walked away on my own, fantasizing.

When I got back home they were all there in the kitchen with Ma. I tried to slip up to my room without being noticed but I wasn't fast enough.

"Where did you get to? People were asking after you. I said you were ill and had gone home," Nick said, why doesn't he keep his great big mouth shut? Ma was there immediately.

"Were you hitching, Peter?"

"I think you mean mitching, Ma, and even that's a bit out of date now."

"Yes, I must try it out in my language sessions. Mitching. Why were you mitching, Peter? Have you got problems? If so I'll ring Wreford Partridge and have a word with him."

"No, no, no," I bawled. "I haven't got any problems. I'm wild with happiness, life's wonderful, everything's fine."

"There's no need to shout, Peter. Just as long as you're sure you don't want me to have a word with . . ."

"The Weevil Bird? No, not that, anything but that. Honestly Ma, I can't bear that."

"The Weevil Bird? I like it," smiled Oliver.

"It's Dad's, not mine."

"He's carrying on a massive test throughout the College." Verna said. "Looks like the usual IQ one to me."

I felt sick. I knew I'd got an IQ in single figures and I didn't want it exposed in all its littleness.

"That's very interesting," Ma came in. "I'll definitely ring up Wreford for I'll be interested in any results he comes up with. How did you get on, Peter? I've always maintained, despite what your father says, that you only fail to fulfil your potential through lack of motivation and concentration. You've probably done quite well."

I thought I should go mad. Oliver stood there smiling, smiling, some time I'll remember that smiling bit. Patronizing berk.

"Let's change the subject," I cried and no one answered. But Willie lurched forward and dropped his coffee all over Kenny. In the hassle I escaped upstairs.

I played a long, long single, that starts slow and quiet, then gets louder and fiercer taking you along with it, alone and free and where I wanted to be, free of them, free of everything, a spirit beyond the struggle, without pain, not stripped and raw and bleeding inside.

PART THREE

———◆———

Scary Monsters (Super creeps)

1

I came out on to the landing. It was very cold. Ma's voice came floating up the stairs, "Why on earth is the front door open?" Then I heard her shout, "Just you come back whoever you are." I ran down the stairs. Mist floated in through the door. Ma stood silhouetted in the doorway and then ran into the street, calling, "Pete, Pete, come on." Two figures were running down the street and she ran after them. It was very early morning and just light as I followed her out on to the front path and they came up all around me like grey animals, dark shapes coming from bushes, walls and behind the trees. There must have been a dozen of them. I thought, "How can I be hated by so many?" and the terror overwhelmed me as Ma turned and shouted, "Look out, Pete. Look out!" and started to run towards me. I jumped back to shut the door against them, but I'd got to wait for Ma, and in that moment they'd surrounded me, one of them pulled the door shut and pushed me against it. I heard Ma screaming as they moved in.

I shoved my feet from under the covers and lay absolutely still, sweat running off me like rain. I hadn't screamed out loud I didn't think. When I was small I often did and Dad would come in, saying the awful row I was making had scared the living daylights out of him and he'd have to stay with me till he felt brave enough to go back to bed. But I hadn't had bad nightmares lately, not since those days at Rolleston Boys when Ben Chapman and his mate Conger had seen it as their daily task to do me over. One day they went too far with a third year kid and the teachers woke up to what was going on. Chapman and Conger disappeared and bullying went out of fashion, for a while. When it revived Willie and I had gone beyond. Funny, I'd almost forgotten that pair, but the nightmare had brought them back. Weird. I reached out for the light and a book, read for a bit and then thought about the girl, my cobweb girl, and fell asleep.

"Why don't you get your mother to call you in the morning? It's almost midday and you're lying there with that look on your face. You haven't got time for that kind of thing. You said you wanted me to come out with you."

"Ma's never got me up nor anyone else for that matter. She has to get through her reading and write six pages before she goes out."

"Tough," said Willie. "My Gran always wakes me, and gives me breakfast."

I crawled under the bed for my socks and got a mouthful of fluff, and eventually surfaced into the daylight.

Half-term break had arrived. The last week had finished with a disco and I'd gone along like a veteran, feeling I'd been going to discos all my life. Quite a lot was happening. Verna and Nick had been elected as first year representatives, and were pretty full of themselves which didn't make much difference as they always were, anyway. They expected to be pretty busy and didn't expect we'd see so much of them. Oliver and Kenny were dropping out, not coming back after the half-term. Oliver had contacts, he said, and was sure he could get them both jobs. But Claire told me they'd done so little work they'd been given an ultimatum by the Principal, work or get out.

"What are the contacts, d'you think?"

"Don't ask me," she answered. "I don't think I want to know. You want to see they don't intend to sit around your

76

place all day long drinking coffee and smoking your Dad's cigarettes. But no, your Dad will throw them out, won't he?''

''He's going right to the north of Scotland for about six weeks, starting Monday. He keeps complaining about it.''

''Still, your Mum won't put up with 'em, will she?''

''I hope not.'' But the trouble was I wasn't sure just what Mum would put up with if she thought it was in a good cause.

I'd persuaded Willie to cycle to the Tower with me. He wasn't keen, especially since he'd been with Claire to a horror film the night before, and dreary outings with me as well as Claire were a bit much, he said. I asked him how he'd got on and he wouldn't tell me anything about it except that it was a horror evening, which I said was unkind as Claire was a very nice person, at which he said that if that was how I felt why didn't I go out with her next time and the best of British luck. At last we managed to get going and arrived at the Tower, where the weather turned stormy, blowing half a gale, tearing the leaves off the trees and exposing the crumbling battlements and flaking plaster, making the building look frail and vulnerable, about to topple down at any minute. There was no sign of the girl. I hadn't really expected there would be. In fact there was no sign of anyone at all, Jeffrey and Humphrey nowhere to be seen, and the place obviously closed for winter hibernation. Willie had an idea they lived in some ancient house deeper in the woods, and I immediately wanted to look for it, but by now we were soaked to the skin by the slanting rain, and Willie turned very morose and peevish, asking why on earth I wanted to hang about this boring old neck of the woods — I hadn't ever said anything about the girl to anyone so he didn't know — and if I wasn't careful I'd turn into one of those nasty old men you read about in the Sunday newspapers who lurk in woods and dark places. And he'd got a sore throat coming.

So we went home, both fed up, and I ate two Chinese take-aways by way of some sort of consolation.

Sal rang up wanting to speak to Ma. She sounded a bit weepy so I asked her what was up and she said that she and Tony had split.

"Great."

"It's easy for you to say that. Get Ma for me."

"She's out photocopying her new book. She's finished it and is starting to research another. I've got a feeling it's about Kenny."

Sal made a disgusted noise at the other end.

"You do seem down."

"I am. Tony's taking out Prue Lennox, my flat mate, you see, only he isn't. Taking her out, I mean. They don't go out, they carry on on the sofa, especially when I'm around."

"Tough. But you're well rid of him."

"Get Dad for me."

"If you want Dad you must be down."

"I'm glad to hear you got rid of that nerd," Dad bellowed down the phone. "No, I don't care if you thought he was handsome. Beauty is only skin deep. Think of your mother. How is she? Dealing with literacy at the prison. Remarkable success rate. They're all reading the Russians and George Eliot out of terror. What's much worse is that she seems to have taken to those appalling mates of Pete's. Revolting it is. I'll swear she's reading fairy tales to one of them, the wide ugly one, I know they're all ugly but this one has gone in for it in a big way. Oh, is that why you've rung up? I wondered why we were wasting all this time jabbering about nothing. No, I don't know where your birth certificate is. I probably threw the horror document away years ago. You're coming to look for it at the weekend? You've only just left home. Why do you want to come back? It's awful here. You can't be fed up. If I say that your mother is cooking rabbit pie for Sunday lunch would that put you off? No? A pity. Look forward to seeing you on Sunday then."

Sal came for the weekend seeming a bit more cheerful. Later she came up to my room. I think she thought I was on my own and she'd come to bring some coffee and have a natter. But the room was full of Oliver, Kenny and smoke.

"Care for a look, Sara?" Oliver asked, smooth and smiling as ever, holding out a porn magazine. Kenny sniggered, as nasty a sound as you're ever likely to hear.

"No thanks, I've seen them all," she replied, cool, cool Sara. "Just you two here?" She made them seem like a couple of cockroaches who'd wandered in by mistake. "Where's Willie?"

"He's got flu."

"Sad." She made her exit, as cold as ice.

After I'd eventually got rid of them, I went downstairs. She looked at me and slitted her eyes, and then turned to Ma who was tut-tutting at the colour supplements, which I think she reads so that she can disapprove of them. I felt very uneasy. Suddenly Sal said,

"Ma, are those two often here? You know, dishonest Oliver and Neanderthal Man?"

"Don't call them that. They've got an awful lot of problems which I'm helping them with."

"I think we'll have an awful lot of problems if they keep coming round here."

"Why do you say that?"

"I just don't trust them."

"Well, I know Kenny isn't quite . . ."

"I'm not being a snob. It's just that they give me the creeps. I know it's not my business any more but I don't think they should come here so often."

"Sara, I'm very surprised at you. You must know, with the upbringing you've had, that it's our duty to help the under-privileged and unemployed of today."

"I can't see how that applies to Oliver!"

Ma had finished the conversation, and had turned back to her reading.

But Sal didn't give up.

"When I was out this afternoon I saw those two hanging about with a terrible-looking mob. You don't want them coming round here, do you?"

"Sara, I think you exaggerate. I'm sure that Oliver and Kenny — I'm growing fond of Kenny, a poor disadvantaged lad if ever I saw one, and Oliver, of course, has real ability, I'm thinking up a course of study for him, he's been so unsettled by those unkind parents of his — I'm absolutely sure that they are good sound material."

"For what? Gaol?"

"Sal, you sound just like my mother, a very harsh woman, I may say. Once she thrashed me and kept me in for a week because I put on some nail varnish. You must become more tolerant in your outlook."

Sal sighed. "I'll have one more go. Do you know they've brought a whole lot of porn mags in here? What next? Drugs? Firearms?"

"I think you're a bit upset, Sal. Perhaps you're overtired. Try to get an early night. And don't worry about the magazines. Oliver lent one to me so that I could have a good laugh."

"Oh, I give up." Sal stormed to the door, where she ran straight into Dad, just coming in. "Look out, though, there'll be trouble with those two!"

Dad said, "If you're talking about Pete's 'orrible mates, I agree. I banned them for life as they went down the path. Hey, don't forget the horror document." He handed the birth certificate to her.

"Oh, thanks." Suddenly she threw her arms round his neck, and kissed him. "You may be mad, but my mother is completely, utterly and dangerously round the twist!"

2

Oliver slithered out of my room followed by Kenny, who had to be woken up first. It was three o'clock in the morning and I was almost past sleeping. The room hung with smoke and I felt terrible. All right for them. They could lie in bed the next day but I'd got a whole lot of sessions including handing in an Economics project for my course work. I was going to finish the last bit off later that evening but I couldn't because they came back after the others had gone home, Claire and Willie, and threw pebbles at my window till I let them in. Ma couldn't hear because she's at the front whereas my room sticks out into the garden at the back. I told them to push off, not till it cools down out there Oliver said, and they sat smoking and listening to records and waited. Nobody said anything. I lay on my bed and looked at the ceiling and waited. I wanted to go to sleep and I couldn't. I didn't know what they'd been up to. I didn't ask and I didn't want to know. I lay there and longed for my old untidy room, my old sanctuary. For I was scared. They scared the wits out of me. They were high as kites, smelling of dope and danger, clever, smiling Oliver and stupid Kenny, whom he'd forged into some sort of weapon. I was scared of them and even more scared of what and who they brought with them, that gang, the hard characters and the fuzz. I thought I knew about fear, but I was acquiring a new dimension, for this was happening all the time.

When did it begin? Being afraid of them? After half-term, I

suppose. Dad went up north, complaining bitterly, and telling Ma he would expect at least three books produced in his absence, and thank the Lord he might get a decent meal. Ma said she was starting an intensive course of study. Sal went on a fortnight's course in management. Verna and Nick were very much involved at College. I started to stay there later and later, but at the end of each day Oliver and Kenny, like leeches, like parasites, like doom awaited me. Always polite to Ma, standing up when she came into a room, making her coffee, offering her cigarettes though she doesn't smoke. They were always at our house. I grew sick of them.

"I think you're jealous," she laughed at me glaring as she lent books to Oliver and showed him how to fill in application forms. She was helping Kenny with his reading.

"Why us?" I moaned to Claire. "Why pick on us?"

"Your mother and father are good cover. Especially your mother. Who'll suspect anyone friendly with her?"

Next, of course they moved in with us, coming to Ma with the story that Oliver hadn't been able to pay his rent because his Social Security wasn't through yet, and Kenny's mother had had a row with him and thrown both him and Kenny out. They'd got Sal's room till my father came back, anyway, or till they'd had time to find somewhere else.

"What are they likely to be suspected of, d'you know?" I asked Claire.

"I don't know. But something will happen."

It seemed to me Claire was the only person I could talk to about how much they scared me. But Claire went down with flu, badly, caught from Willie who'd had it mildly after the Tower outing.

One night he and I were coming back home slowly from the pictures, wandering through the High Street eating chips and looking in the record shops before we went home, and as we passed the Crown and Anchor the door opened and a whole lot of blokes shot out as if catapulted. And spotted us.

Then one cried, "Let's get 'em," and they came after us. For no reason. Nightmare time had come. Dropping the chips we fled down the street and round the corner, two of them right behind us, so we dodged down a narrow alley that cuts through to our street, Willie running like a greyhound just out of the trap, ahead of me on his longer legs, but I'm going like the clappers and catching him up for those behind are yelling about what they'll do to us when they get us and it's not pretty at all. We raced around a corner, then jumped over a garden wall and crouched behind it, hidden, I hoped, by a bush.

And they rushed past.

The running footsteps died away. Cautiously, painfully we stood up. Safe. We climbed back over the wall, slowly this time, breathing heavily, and dropped down on to the pavement.

"I didn't know you went in for that kind of thing," said a voice softly and then Kenny loomed over me, while Oliver smiled, and it was not at all a sight I wanted to see on the night streets.

"Ma wouldn't like to know that you'd been out doing the neighbourhood, would she? I know there are villains who go in for that kind of thing but not her dear little Peterkin. She is in for a surprise."

Kenny didn't say anything. He just thumped me playfully and it hurt. Part of me was registering that they were coming out into the open at last, but it didn't give me much satisfaction.

"Don't mind him," purred Oliver. "That's how he communicates. He's not very articulate, are you, Kenny?"

"Hey, don't do that," yelled Willie, as Kenny decided to communicate with him as well.

"You know we haven't been doing anything, Oliver. We

jumped over that wall to get out of the way of those hooligans.''

''What hooligans?''

''That crowd of madmen rushing past. They were chasing us. For no reason. You must have seen them.''

''They made me drop my chips,'' Willie complained.

''I didn't see any hooligans but it's as good a story as any. But you don't expect anyone to believe it, do you?''

''It's true,'' Willie cried.

''I won't give you away. And Kenny here never says a dicky bird, do you, Kenny? I won't say that there wasn't anyone after you or anything like that. Not if you cut us in on what you've picked up tonight.''

''We haven't got anything and you know it, Oliver. Come on, Willie. Let's get going. No use standing here arguing.''

Kenny seized Willie's hand and twisted it till it opened and I got mad. I rushed at Kenny and kicked him in the shin and was immediately filled with terror. That's done it, I thought, as he turned towards me like a great, shambling bear.

''Leave it, Kenny,'' said Oliver. ''It doesn't matter. See you, Pete, Willie. Any chance of the lovely Sara coming home this weekend?''

Willie nursed his hand, eyes full of hatred.

Later that evening, when they'd invited themselves into my room, ''My friends,'' Oliver murmured gently, ''liked what I told them about your house, didn't they, Kenny? They liked what I told them about your Ma, how kind she is to us. They liked it a lot. And I said to them, didn't I Kenny, that it was unfortunate that your Dad was away up north just now as it would be most distressing if anything happened to your old dear, if she was hurt or the house done over while he wasn't here. They said that they'd help keep an eye on it, for a few small favours. Is this a new album, Pete? Good, isn't it? May I borrow it?''

And so I started to be afraid, really afraid, though half of me couldn't believe it was happening, for it was all so corny, so tenth rate B movie. I'd only got to tell someone. But who? Willie and Ma were the only ones around at the moment, and Willie was even more scared of them than I was. Dad on the phone? Not easy. He'd think I'd gone barmy. Sometimes I thought so, too. The police, tell the fuzz? What had I got to tell? I didn't like the blokes staying with us — I thought they were trouble? No, all I could do was wait. But the nightmares were very bad.

"I like that one," said Aunt Sybil, when she came round one evening. "Such a neat, quiet boy. And he takes care of the other one. What's his name? Peter? Answer me."

"I'm sorry, I wasn't listening, Aunt."

"There. Exactly like his father. No manners. I do think a pleasant manner is so important."

Next time she came she'd found some jobs for them to do at her house and in the garden, she said. I nearly said, don't let them near the place, they'll only be sussing it out for the gang, but I didn't. After all, as far as Aunt Sybil could see they were always in our house so obviously they were friends. They'd pretend to go to bed, go out, return in the small hours and talk in my room till I wanted to go mad, Ma never hearing a thing at the front, in our old, tall house.

"Write to your Dad," said Willie. "He'll settle them. Your Dad'd settle anything. After all, I can't tell my Gran, can I?"

"What do I write, then? 'Dear Dad, I am writing to you because I think that Ma and I are in danger. Your son, Peter.'"

I didn't think Dad would take kindly to that at all, especially since from the calls Ma had he seemed to be horribly busy. And I know he's always thought I was the world's wettest heap and after reading that he'd be sure of it, Daddy dear, come home, we're scared without you, at least I am. I didn't know about Ma. She didn't seem ever to think about things like being

85

afraid, always too busy on education or ideas or protesting. I just knew I didn't like the idea of her being menaced by Oliver and all those merry men

I went to see Claire who was feeling better but not allowed out yet.

"Don't be daft. You'll have to tell your mother. Tell her straight and then she'll understand . . ."

"I didn't tell anyone when I was bullied at school . . ."

"More fool you, then. And this is different. She's got a right to know about people in her house. Get her to tell them to find somewhere else to live. Wait till they let me out and I'll come with you. I know you find it hard explaining things. Hey, you're actually grinning. What have you found to grin about?"

"All my life I wanted Dad and Ma to leave me alone a bit, take no notice of me as I made a mess of everything. And it's happened. They're not taking a blind bit of notice of me and I want to yell at them, 'Look at me. Look at me. I'm going mad.'"

3

When I got in Aunt Sybil was there talking like a pneumatic drill buzzing on and on. The house next door, and next door to her means quite a distance away because the houses on the hill where she lives are big with massive grounds, had been burgled and an immense quantity of stuff taken by a gang that knew what they were doing, and she was very frightened was Aunt Sybil, she'd had all her burglar alarms checked and was thinking of getting a guard dog, and if dear Vincent, that's my uncle, was ever away, she'd get someone to sleep there, perhaps Sal or Oliver, Peter being a bit young. And useless was in brackets though she didn't say so.

Ma gave her gin and sympathy, but I knew her mind was really on getting away as she wanted to do some work and hates wasting time with Sybil, and probably because burglaries don't worry her too much as long as somebody doesn't get hurt, Ma having a low opinion of too many material possessions, unlike her dear sister Sybil.

Amazed at the mere idea of Oliver as a minder in Aunt Sybil's house, I picked up the local paper, an awful rag that I never look at except to see what's on at the cinema or what our third division team is doing, and it appeared to be full of crimes, somebody always busy somewhere all of the time, probably the gang for much of it. Full of deep gloom I wandered upstairs and put on a record and was just getting lost in it when in they walked — which was another thing I hated — I'd never had a lock on my door, it hadn't been needed much for we weren't people who walked in and out all the time, but the hateful duo did. Kenny was carrying something, a very expensive Japanese calculator, for you, Oliver said, we brought you a prezzy.

I stared at it as if it was lethal, and shook my head.

"Thanks, but I like to know my prezzies haven't dropped off the back of a lorry or something similar."

"Fancy you not trusting us. Kenny, teach him about trust."

Kenny biffed me without malice. It still hurt. I kicked him back, then lay back on the bed and hated. It was all old, familiar and boring and horrible.

"Did you hear from Aunt Sybil that it's all happening?" asked Oliver.

"Yes, I did. Look, I've got work to do. Push off, will you?"

"We might, we might. If you give us something to go with."

"Look, you know I get very little money, and what I do get, you take off me, anyway."

"Ma's very generous with hers, leaves little bits and pieces lying around. There's a couple of quid been lying on the sideboard for a day or two. I think she's forgotten them as usual. Fetch 'em for me, Peterkin, and Kenny and I'll take ourselves off."

And I got the pound notes, as usual, and hated myself. Not that Ma would make trouble or even notice, she thinks so little of money that she's very absent-minded about it. But I minded. I put on my favourite record, the wild one, and listened, and thought about how I'd decided that something was gonna change, especially me, and how at first, I'd thought things were changing and getting better, now the only change was for the worse. Even the work was going off. Joe had called me back the other day. "Lost interest?" he asked. I shook my head. "Problems? Don't forget I'm here to be harassed." But I only shook my head again, and promised to give in the essay that was already a week overdue.

Somehow I finished it, knowing it wasn't any good. I picked up the calculator left by Kenny, and wondered if it had come from that burglary or just shoplifting. Either way I'd need to get it out of sight. I pushed it behind some old paperbacks. And I wondered why, if they were involved with the big time like Rieber's gang, they needed a miserable couple of quid?

I went to the mirror and peered in it. A spotty face with scruffy tufts of beard peered back at me, not a pretty sight. No wonder I was so feeble looking like that. I'd go and see Willie. We wandered round the town for ages, going to the amusement arcade — Willie had some cash, I hadn't — drinking coffee, back to the amusement arcade again. And playing the machines I decided quite suddenly, out of the blue, that I was going to speak to Ma.

All the way home, I rehearsed what I was going to say, getting it clear, so that I didn't sound like some sort of wet drip, but taking the common-sense point of view, such as they stay so late at night that I'm knackered and I can't keep up with my work, at which of course she could well say, but you've never in the whole of your life kept up with your work to which really there could be no answer. Oh, I'll just say what comes into my head, I thought, and then maybe she'll tell them to go away, I hope.

But as it happened, the conversation between me and Ma about getting rid of Oliver and Kenny didn't take place at all.

I knew they were CID men. Don't ask me how. I just knew. They wore neat suits, had dark hair, greying a little, and one was older than the other. They sat in the front room, and Ma was serving them tea and biccies. She looked happy. I suppose if your life has been filled with chapel going three times daily when you were young, and you've spent ever since trying to improve the world you don't feel ill when the fuzz turn up.

I did though. I tried to vamoose quick, to slide backwards out of the door that I'd been foolish enough to open in the first place.

"Don't go away, Peter, dear. Come in and say, Hello. This is my son. He's at the Sixth Form College. Peter, these men, who belong to the CID, have called to ask some questions, and I expect you'd like to help as well."

Oh, no, no, please this couldn't happen to a dog.

"I'll leave you alone, Ma," I said.

"No need. It's all right. Just listen, Peter. You might be helpful."

I doubted it. The mere look of these two large men paralysed me. So did the word help. Why did Ma keep using it? What did she mean? What it meant to me was connected with that well-known phrase "helping with their enquiries" and whatever that implied.

They asked if we could remember whether Oliver and Kenny were with us on the previous Monday evening. I hadn't the faintest idea. But Ma remembered. Yes, apparently they were. They had watched a film following the nine o'clock news, and gone out about eleven. She'd remembered particularly because she'd come downstairs from working and checked that they'd closed the door properly.

"I didn't want any burglars coming in," she laughed.

The CID men didn't laugh. "The burglars were probably already inside and just leaving," one remarked heavily.

"Surely not," she said. "Not those two poor boys. What are they supposed to have done?"

"We are making enquiries into a number of break-ins in the area. However," he continued, his voice even heavier, "you have confirmed their alibi. So now they are in the clear."

90

The police got up to go, to my relief. Then I realized that if Ma had failed to confirm Oliver's and Kenny's alibi, they might have got into serious trouble. And gone away, I thought. I might never have seen them again. What a lovely idea. Still, perhaps my words with Ma would now carry more weight. The older of the two men was saying.

"Excuse me, but if you don't mind a little advice from us, we wouldn't have those two, Oliver especially, in our houses, and we recommend that you shouldn't have them here. They're bound to give you trouble sooner or later."

"Why do you say that?"

"Because they're trouble-makers, and totally untrustworthy. They've been known to us for some time and if you've any sense, ma'am, you'll not let them have the run of your house." Oh, brilliant, I thought.

Ma had gone red all up her neck and her eyes were flashing.

"Do you realize that it's November? That it's cold and dark outside, that they've no money and nowhere to go? If they are among life's casualties, then I shall be the last to thrust them forth. While they are in my house, watching television and drinking coffee, they are up to no harm. Someone has to take them in. Otherwise they are doomed."

"As far as I'm concerned that one's doomed anyway. There isn't an honest bone in his body. And he's cruel."

I nodded mentally in agreement. This copper had got the pair weighed up nicely, but Ma wasn't having any. Like St. George fighting the dragon she charged on.

"They will always be welcome here. I shall take care of them. Goodbye and thank you for calling."

She made them sound as if they were selling things at the door, which she closed behind them in a satisfied way.

"Ma, are you sure you're right?"

"Goodness and charity are always right," she said. I shut up lest she break into "Onward Christian Soldiers", a pacifist version, of course, and went upstairs, feeling sick, very sick. Dad would be surprised to receive a telegram that read, "Ma flipped her lid. Come home." But perhaps I was exaggerating it all. Now that Oliver knew the police were interested in him surely he'd keep a very low profile. Somehow I couldn't worry any more. I'd had enough. I picked out an old Punk record by the Stranglers. Its haunting and spooky music gave me some sort of hope, a courage to survive. I sank deeper and deeper into it and tried to forget everything but the sound rising and falling. At last, I thought of the girl, the cobweb girl, and thinking about her I went to sleep.

4

I handed in various bits of work, some overdue. Then I went to see Nick, who was having coffee with Verna and discussing union affairs as I guessed they would be.

"Nick, I'm getting pretty sick of having Oliver and Kenny hanging about our house as they're a nuisance and sponging off me. I wondered what you would do about it, as you're good at dealing with problems and so on, and you brought them along in the first place. I feel I got landed and wondered what you would do in my case."

"Ah, I'm glad you came to me," he said, pleased as I thought he would be, particularly with "problems", I'd heard several students say that Nick was good at handling problems. "D'you want to leave it with me?"

"Not especially. They could say it was none of your business what they do in our house, y'see."

"Mm. Tricky. What do you think, Verna?"

"I've missed you, Peterkin. Have you been miserable without me?"

"I've been miserable. Don't know if it was because I was without you."

Verna put her head on one side. "You want Oliver and Kenny out? I tell you what I'd do. I'd ring Sara. Get her to deal with 'em. I think she's fabulous. Did you hear her at that last meeting?"

Nick didn't want to hear what Sal had said at that last meeting.

"Oliver's a tricky customer. Needs a bloke to deal with him. I'm not sure Sal could manage it . . ."

"You sexist pig . . ." said Verna. "How I dislike you."

"Nothing to do with what we're talking about. No, Pete, the best person to tell is your Dad. I don't suppose you've thought of that, but that's your best bet. He'd get rid of anything."

"He's away."

"Ring him up then. Nothing could be easier. And I'll call in one night and let 'em know they could go somewhere else. Sorry I haven't been round lately. Now, Verna, what about the 8th? Will that do?"

"I dunno. See you, Peterkin, and don't worry. We'll have another disco soon, and you can dance with me."

I walked away.

"I tell you what," Willie put in. I hadn't known he was there as well, listening. "It makes it clear how wonderful Sal is."

"What does?" I asked, baffled but not surprised, for Willie could turn anything into Sal-worship.

"All the things she's done, she's always just the same. Whereas those two, well, are conceited twits, full of themselves."

"I couldn't care less. I'm going to the library. See you over in the Waste Land."

"Pete."

"Yes?"

"Sal doesn't seem to be going out with anyone just now . . ."

"How would we know? She might be in and out of bed with guys like a yo-yo, for all we know, since she's not here."

"I wondered if she'd go out with me, since I don't think there's anyone else."

I looked at Willie, an elongated Brer Rabbit without the cunning wit, and thought it highly unlikely, but he was my friend . . . my real friend, and said,

"Give it a go, and I'll put in a word for you. Now, I must go."

Strangely enough, feeling quite cheerful, I ran along the corridor, and there, there she was. She was for real, she was for real. I hadn't imagined her, dreamt her up. She existed. And she did come to the College. There she stood in the corridor, my cobweb girl, and the wild melody sang in my head like glory.

There was a problem (there always is). She was deep in conversation with the Weevil Bird. And looking worried. Of course, anyone would look worried talking to the Weevil Bird. It wouldn't be a thing you'd want to do, would it? Be in conversation with the Weevil Bird. And remembering that test I didn't do I had no desire that the Weevil Bird should lay eyes or his third eye on me. So I backtracked and lurked behind a bend in the corridor, poking my head out at intervals and hoping not to be noticed, waiting for the Weevil Bird to finish and rehearsing a thousand witty opening phrases. But a vast multi-chinned woman of great cheer and enormous learning bore down on me. It was the History tutor.

"Bates" — she always calls me Bates. "Carry these to the library for me, will you please."

These were an enormous pile of books standing on a table round the corner. I could have wept.

"Don't hang about, you'll manage them easily. Stout fellow. That's it. I'll lead the way for you in case you can't see over the top."

When I arrived back at the spot, the sacred spot in the corridor where her feet had stood, she'd gone, of course. Sweaty, smelling and near tears I stood there waiting, but she'd gone.

Dad rang. Ma had gone out to a meeting. And here was my opportunity. I took a deep breath and decided to tell him that things were in a mess at this end. Dad's not the easiest of people to tell things to and I never find talking on the phone much fun either, but this time I'd do it. Sort it all out.

Oliver stood in the hall smiling at me. He'd come in quietly through the back door and walked up behind me. My flesh crept. He could easily have stuck a knife in my back, I thought wildly. Then Kenny joined him and they leaned on the wall on either side of me like listening bookends.

"Everything OK?" asked my father.

"Fine."

I'm in a trap, I'm in a trap, I was screaming inside.

"How is your mother? Seething with manic energy as usual, I suppose?"

"She's fine."

"You'd better tell her I miss her, I suppose. We can't have her turning peculiar. Or more peculiar than she is already. Excellent cooking up here by the way. I haven't had indigestion for a fortnight. Remember to get up each day, Pete. That's the general idea. Stick to that and you can't go far wrong, even you. Goodbye. Thank you for talking to me. Are you there, by the way, or have you gone away?"

"Yes. I am here, I mean."

"Goodbye."

I looked at the bookends. Oliver was smiling. I was as full of hatred as an orange of juice.

"The fuzz came round for you."

"Yes, I've been to the station. They couldn't prove anything. They had to let me go." He shrugged.

"Ma gave you an alibi. That's why."

"Yes, I just met her. She's offered to come with me if it happens again, to see I get fair treatment. Don't look so miserable, Peterkin. How about making us a nice cup of coffee?"

I thought of all the coffee, food, cigarettes, albums, paper-backs, cans of lager and Dad's whisky all going steadily in their direction.

"Make it yourself. I've got work to do."

I went upstairs and wedged my door shut. Tomorrow I'd buy a bolt and put it on the door. Then I put on an album at full blast so that it pounded at my head and my ears and my eyes and my body, the wild sounds roaring and throbbing and screaming their way into my brain so that the anger and fear and hatred swirled and sang and wailed its sorrow then ebbed away and died in quiet despair and everything was silent. I went out on to the landing. From the landing window you can climb out on to the roof and I sat there for a long time staring at the stars and the lights down below and the thin bare branches of trees etched against the night sky.

It must have been about two when Kenny pushed his great weight against my door and despite the chair being there it opened, and in they came. I shoved my head under the clothes but Kenny hauled me out. They were high again, boasting and laughing. I didn't listen, kept trying to blank off, but I gathered that while I'd been sitting on the roof, they'd been doing something, somewhere, and were talking about how to dispose of the stuff, most of which they'd apparently dumped around our house. A large bag was shoved inside one of my cup-boards. "Le Big Job," laughed Oliver. And, "You'll hear about it tomorrow," Kenny said.

"Why are you telling me all this?" I'd asked. "I don't want to know. And you might just push me too far and I'll end up telling someone."

Kenny pulled a knife out of his pocket and sprang it open.

"Don't," he said.

"Always so dramatic, dear Kenny," Oliver smiled.

97

It was all so second rate, so stupid. But there was nothing second rate about my terror. That was in a premier class.

I tried to call up my cobweb girl for sleeping. But she was far away, very distant.

5

Ma was working in her room and the other two were still in bed, of course, as I tuned into our local radio programme, just in time for the news, and there it was, daring break-in, wealthy local business man's palatial home, Latimer Hill (near Aunt Sybil), many valuables stolen, insured for thousands, oh, Lord, even worse than I'd thought, well organized, it said, unbelievable. I switched off. What on earth was I going to do? Tell Ma and the fuzz, of course. Then I remembered Kenny's knife and the stuff stashed all over our house. It wasn't easy, not straightforward at all. But I'd obviously got to do something, talk to somebody. I sat and waited for Willie, brain churning like a mouse on a treadwheel. At last I looked at the clock. Willie was late, very late, and so was I. I'd better get a move on if I wasn't to be late for History, and that female tutor would obliterate me, calling me Bates as she did so. I rushed out of the house.

And continued rushing. It was one of those days. I was called hither and yon, given messages, called back for natters, sent on errands, all the while looking out for Nick and Verna whom I desperately wanted to see, coming across them at last at lunch-time in the coffee bar, surrounded by people. Music was playing, the noise was terrible.

"Yes, I know it's time we had a party," shouted Verna. "The question is where . . . Peterkin. Darling Peterkin. Darling Peterkin." She hurled herself upon me, and I sagged at the knees. Had she been drinking, I wondered? No, she was just being Verna.

"I've remembered something, all of you. None of you know, and I bet he doesn't know that I know, do you, Peterkin?"

"Know what?" I asked, trembling, my nerves in shreds, what did she know, awful girl, why had I hoped for help here?

"It's your birthday this week. You see, I've remembered. Bet you thought I'd forgotten. But I remember coming to your parties when you were a little boy. You always cried and hid in a corner, and then you'd go mad and rush out and bite somebody and scream . . ."

"Thank you, Verna."

"You're welcome. A party at Pete's house, everybody. I'll ask his Mum. She'll be all right."

"It's a big house. We can do a disco."

"Food. Lashings of food."

"Drink's more important."

"Lights. I'll fix the lights."

"Fancy dress?"

"Why not fancy dress?"

"Anything."

"Nothing you mean. Even better."

"We'll invite everybody."

"It'll be great."

"It'll be fantastic."

They'd all gone mad. Like Dad I'd been speaking for some time. The difference was people listen to Dad and this lot weren't listening to me. There was a brief hush. I was in with a chance.

"There's just one thing," I bellowed. They even turned to listen. "I don't want a party. I don't WANT A PARTY!"

The noise rose and hit the walls and roof. No one was taking a blind bit of notice of me.

A notice on the door said the Maths tutor had flu, would we just carry on with work for the time being. I was fairly sure that Oliver and Kenny would be out of the house by now, and I cut back home. I wanted a zizz more than anything. I was knackered. I fell on the bed and was lost to the whole wide world. Eventually the door bell ringing and ringing roused me and I went downstairs. Willie stood there. He looked rotten.

"They've done our house, Pete," he said.

I let him in and we went into the kitchen.

"Your Gran?"

"She's all right. Claire's with her. You were right. She is a nice girl."

I made him some coffee. He didn't cry, and I don't think I could have stood it if Willie had cried. But he sat there, his eyes somehow dead, his face drained. He repeated that his Gran was all right but very upset, and the police had been and they'd told them what they knew which wasn't a lot. Whoever it was must have got in about twelve last night after they'd gone to bed. They hadn't taken much, a cassette player of Willie's, a purse with about a fiver in it, and a small radio. But they'd broken things and helped themselves to food in the kitchen. It was a wonder they hadn't been heard.

"Do you think it was that gang Oliver knows?" I asked.

"I dunno."

"They did something last night. They were boasting. Then I listened to the radio and thought they'd been mixed up in that job on Latimer Hill."

"Perhaps they did that as well," Willie said wearily.

"They sound rather different efforts. Willie!"

"What?"

"They shoved something at the back of my cupboard. Suppose it's your cassette. Let's go and look."

Two minutes later we were staring at the contents of a poly-thene bag. It was full of watches and biros.

101

"I wish Sal was here. Why don't you ring her up? Have you got her number?"

"Yes, but she won't be in. Not at this time. She'll be at one of her meetings or something."

"Try," said Willie.

Sal's number was written over the phone along with Dad's. I dialled it and waited, and she spoke.

"Pete. Whatever. I've never known you ring me up. I was just going out."

"Sal."

"What's wrong?"

"Nothing. I mean everything."

She sounded not anxious, no, urgent, Sal's getting things done voice,

"It's the last session tomorrow. Then I'm coming. Hold on, and don't worry."

Willie looked better, even smiled a bit, pleased she was coming back.

"I'll get back to my Gran," he said. "I've got some bits and pieces at College. Could you pick them up for me, Pete, and find out what I've missed out on, today?"

"Sure."

"See you."

It was getting dark as I walked up the wooden stairs to the Waste Land room. The students were gone, but Joe was still there, marking. It felt like home, like my old room used to, before Oliver and Kenny made it into the real waste land. Oliver had suggested that I get hold of Ma's Service card and lend it to him, you'll easily find out the number and she'll never notice, he'd said. Better to lose a few pounds from the bank than have the place done over by the gang, he'd said, because the lads are messy at times, their ways are not pretty, they weren't brought up nicely like you and me, Peterkin. Kenny's still a bit rough at times, aren't you, Kenny? And Kenny had twisted my arms a few times to show me that he was still a bit rough.

I was half-way through this when I realized what I was telling Joe sitting there in the room, the sky darkening outside the windows.

"It's dark out there, Joe," I said.

"Yes, it is, Pete, very dark at times. But it does get light as well, a fifty-fifty operation, pretty fair. Is that what happened to the work?"

"Yes. Sorry. I couldn't cope. I've always been a bit feeble."

"I think I'd 've been a bit feeble, as well. Tell me the rest."

"It's not epic stuff, it's petty and stupid, my troubles are rubbish. But to me they're real. There was only one fatal casualty, reads the newscaster, but it was just as fatal for him as if there'd been hundreds."

A student poked its head in, sorry, and went away. A sudden roar went up from the room next door. Someone was putting on a good performance.

Joe waited. It was peaceful in that room.

"Take your time," he said.

When I'd finished he said,

"We must warn your mother."

"She didn't listen to the CID."

"Who would she listen to?"

Somewhere outside a light was switched on, a girl laughed, a happy sound.

"She's a friend of the . . . Principal's." I'd remembered in time not to say Weevil Bird.

"Right. Go home and stop worrying so much. Did I hear something about a party on the grapevine?"

"Party? Oh, yes, that. Verna wants to have one at my house. For my birthday."

"Why don't you? You might enjoy it, you never know."

I wandered through the College looking for people to talk to but they'd nearly all gone home by now. I walked through rooms and corridors I never knew existed into strange areas, exotic as tropical fruit to me, alien worlds.

There in front of me was the computer room, Claire's pride and joy, where she made programs, fought war games. She'd wanted to take me there but computers meant little to me so I hadn't bothered. But now I wanted to know. I pushed at the door. It would probably be locked at this hour, they were very fussy with the room, she said, and everything was timetabled. But it wasn't locked. I walked in.

She sat there alone, working, while the television screens flickered. I had a chance to look at her before she turned round and saw me. She wasn't like a cobweb, she was like a soft grey cloud.

What did it matter if I was a little guy? So was Cagney, so was Bogart, so was Napoleon, I think, so I walked up to her and I was all of them.

"I'm having a party tomorrow night," I said, just like that, never a stutter, never a hitch. "I'd like you to come. Please."

She stared at me. She had very large grey eyes, and her face looked rumpled and worried. Then she grinned and all the worry went away.

"You're the funny one who trod on the specs. I've been looking out for you. Oh, I'd love to come. Thanks."

6

An avalanche of words poured from Ma, snap, crackle, pop, crash, bang, wallop, slam; injustice, youth, harassment, society, chances, system flew across the room. She pulled on her boots and coat as she spoke.

"I thought it was only your Dad could carry on like that," said Claire, amazed.

"No. They both do. That's why I hardly ever speak."

Ma flew out of the house.

"I bet she beats the fuzz with her broomstick," Nick said, and was frowned on by Verna. "You're so rude, MCP that you are."

"Oh, let's get on, anyway. Blow them."

"I hope the fuzz keep them there. For ever," snapped Claire.

"So do I," added Willie.

It was my birthday. Ma gave me a copy of *The Ragged Trousered Philanthropists* and said she'd pay for the party grub, though she couldn't be there as Wreford Partridge wanted to have a chat about something or other and had asked her over for a meal, but she wouldn't be late back and anyway Sal was due to arrive some time, she'd rung up, sounded a bit odd, Ma thought. I listened to none of that as my stomach was riding a Big Dipper at the mention of the sacred name. Had Joe spoken to him? Sometimes I wished I hadn't said anything to him, especially late last night when Oliver and Kenny came in and Kenny handed me this gold Sheaffer pen, picked out specially from the best shop in town, he said. Oliver said he'd got me a prezzy as well, only we were going to play Treasure Hunt with this one. Somewhere in the house he'd hidden some pot and if I breathed a word to anyone especially the fuzz, then he'd tell them where it was in our house and that I'd put it there. That's when I regretted talking to Joe. I told them I'd tell Dad when he came back home and Kenny laughed.

"We'll be far away by then, the job's finished," smiled Oliver.

Now in the midst of getting ready for the party Willie and I were searching for a small parcel, we imagined, but we didn't actually know what we were looking for. I'd told Willie, but no one else, for he too, was involved.

In the meantime there I was with a party and jollifications, the birthday boy, cried Verna, kissing me and giving me a single, Number One in the charts for the last four weeks, absolutely horrible, I hated it, fantastic I said, thanks a lot. Nick and Verna had spread the word about the party and people were certainly coming they said. A dream, it was all a dream, for she was coming, but it was a nightmare as well.

People arrived to help, clearing furniture, fixing music and lights. Ma sent us, Nick, Kenny, Oliver and me, into town to get food and drinks, plastic cups and paper plates. Nick talked.

As we walked away from Sainsburys hands dropped on Oliver's and Kenny's shoulders. We all swung round and it was the fuzz. There, just like that, just like all the films I've watched on television, only it was in our High Street and for real. In a daze I waited for them to take me too, but they just walked Kenny and Oliver away.

"We want you to come down to the station with us," they said and walked away from Nick and me, leaving us with the bags of shopping and Nick's mouth wide open. I shall be sick I thought, while my mind whirled and leapt. They'd gone, they'd been taken away, without my doing anything if you didn't count telling Joe. They'd gone. I couldn't believe it. Maybe, maybe it was all over. Kenny had looked back at me, piteously, as he went, but I didn't care, not after what he'd done to me, I didn't care at all, why should I?

"I can't believe it," Nick said slowly. "I wonder what Oliver will tell them. After all, what have they done?"

I don't think he expected to be answered and anyway my mind had stuck on "I wonder what Oliver will tell them," a needle in a groove. Oliver, lying Oliver, what would he say? How long before the police marched me away, wanted me for questioning at the station? How long? And what would I say? What could I say?

"Let's get back and tell your mother," said Nick. It was all we could do.

That's when Ma started to speak and then fly out of the house.

"Get on without me!" she cried and we did just that.

The day went on and on for ever and ever, totally unreal. We got things ready, then played cards and Mastermind and chess, and watched television, and played Cluedo and Monopoly, and chose all the music, and drank coffee and ate fish and chips and waited and waited and waited. At least they all did, I was searching like a madman to find the confounded pot and dispose of it somewhere, anywhere. In the room that once was Sal's, I found watches and pens and transistors and gear, all the consumer goods Ma gets so mad about. Her poor lads had tons of stuff. What should I do with it all? I thought of putting it into a rubbish bag and shoving it out in the back alley ways where the dustbins are kept, but it didn't seem like a very bright idea. In the end I left it there. But I wanted to find the pot parcel or whatever it was and get rid of that.

Willie kept on about Sal coming back. He seemed to think that if she came everything would be all right. I was going to laugh at him, then stopped and thought for the first time that Willie had real feelings — that he wasn't a long, thin joke — and so if he felt about Sal like I did about the girl then it was important to him that she came back soon.

We waited for Ma to return with or without the pair, the others sure she would return alone, but then they didn't know Ma as I did. Beyond all this I waited for the girl, kicking myself for not asking her name or where she lived, for I had no way of contacting her.

Still Ma did not come and at last Verna and Claire stirred and said they were going home to change.

7

What I'd forgotten was how the music would take over. It swept me with it, a huge wave that dipped and surged round and down, under and over the beat, and the music is the sea and the sky, the sun and the wind, the dark and the light, music is the earth and the music is me and I am the music. The lights changed from emerald to turquoise, from turquoise to blue, from blue to amber and to red. Almost, I am happy. Almost.

Claire seizes me in her powerful grip and bounces me up and down to a beat of her own invention. As far as I could see she wears the shortest skirt ever in a mind-blowing pink with hair like Neapolitan ice cream. I've gone. I can't think. I can't see, I'm blowing my mind, my little, tiny mind. Not that it matters for Nick is running everything, the great Nick is Boss, in Complete Control. All I have to worry about is the girl coming. All, all you have to worry about, you twit? What about . . . ? Well, what about them, then? Stuff 'em. Stuff 'em, stuff 'em, stuff 'em. You've worried enough about them to last a lifetime. They can stay where they are. Enjoy yourself, Pete lad, they're where they belong. And Dad'll soon be back, then everything will be all right. Welcome home, Dad.

I keep going to answer the door bell in case she's on the doorstep, and I mustn't miss her. What shall I say? But don't fall over your feet, Pete, don't fall over your feet. Not this time. Stay upright for once. Be a man. Oh, yes, yes, I'd like the chance. A girl kisses me.

"It's a great party," she yells. "You're lovely."

"Do I know you?" I ask.

"No. I came with Paddy. It's a birthday party I think. Sara Williams's little brother. Do you know Sara?"

"No."

"You ought to. She's great."

"Scuse me, I can hear the door bell."

It wasn't her. Verna puts her arms round me, crooning in my ear, "Didn't you do well, Peterkin?" and kisses my ear.

"You've got a thing about ears," I shout.

"Only yours," she cries and leaps into the middle of the floor again, a tawny lioness dancing and pawing the ground.

Claire is singing, "It's my party and I'll cry if I want to . . ."

"Cry if I want to, cry if I want to . . ." I join in. "It's not your party, it's mine . . . and I'll definitely cry if I want to . . ." and everybody laughs, I'm funny.

"Food in the kitchen," shouts Nick. All the time I've known him he's been giving somebody orders. But I don't mind. I'll go to the door again. It's not late. There's plenty of time.

More and more people arrive. Half the College is here. But not her. Not yet. But she'll come. She has to come.

Willie struggles to me. "Is Sal here yet? No. What about your mother? And them?"

"Not here. Sal'll come. You can always trust old Sal. And I don't want *them* to come."

"I wanted to dance with her."

"There's lots of time. Claire, Willie wants a dance with you."

"Lovely! Come on. This is one of my favourites." He goes under protest.

Willie, slow to get going, is now really gone, writhing and swaying to the beat, sweat dripping off him. I roam around just

110

in case she's already here and among the couples and the crisps and the plastic cups on the stairs and the landing. Good thing Dad isn't here. He'd go spare. Claire is weaving towards me, probably wants to throw me round the room again. But the door bell rings and I go to open it, and she's there. With Joe Greenaway, and another girl.

"Hello. Hope we're not gatecrashing, Liz and me, that is. I know Midge was definitely invited," he said.

She was smiling at me. "Come in, come in." I wasn't sure I was quite up to trying out her name. But I did.

"Midge," I said.

"Mm, it's short for midget," she grinned and stared round. "It's lovely. I hardly ever go to parties as my Dad's an old fusspot, but I knew he'd be all right if it was at your house."

I hadn't a clue to what she was talking about but it didn't matter. She'd come. Midge, what a . . . daft name. I liked it.

"Would you like a drink? Something to eat?" I gulped.

But she wanted to dance. Heaven must be a place of stress, I thought. I was happy, madly happy, if only I didn't have two left feet, misty glasses and BO. At last we sat down and I went to get her a drink and was grabbed by Nick, who always knows everything.

"How d'you manage that, eh? Pete the dark horse."

"I don't know what you're talking about."

"Ho, ho, ho. Didn't you do well?"

I pushed past him just as he was seized by Verna, good, serve him right, and then forgot him as Midge and I talked; the two old boys at the Tower were her uncles, her mother's brothers, and she was very fond of them, often went there, she reminded them of her mother who died, she said, a long time ago, not to be sad about it and her father was great but perhaps she didn't get about as much as some girls, lovely I breathed, thinking of the girls I knew always getting about everywhere, and then forgetting them fast. As we talked the party was really getting

111

under way all around us and it was some time before I heard the phone ringing in competition with the Rolling Stones still getting no satisfaction after all these years. As I went to answer it I saw Nick and Verna wrapped round each other in the hall, oh, of course, of course, it was obvious, really, and picked up the phone.

A banshee screamed and wailed at the other end.

"That must be Peter," it cried. "For Heaven's sake get me someone with some sense. Where's Margaret? Your mother, fool. Why is it so noisy? A party? Oh, fetch me Sara before I go insane. They're out? I must get hold of them. I've been burgled!"

"Oh no! Wait, she's just come in!"

And following Ma was a short, balding man in hairy tweeds. Oh well, the end. I needed the Weevil Bird here like I needed a hole in the head. Did he always go to his students' birthday parties I wondered wildly, busy man? Ma came to the phone and the Weevil Bird bore down on me as I retreated back to my girl. She and I could tremble together. He kept following me and turned to Midge with an unbelievably sweet smile — a different man.

"Having a good time, Midge? You know Peter, of course, Margaret's son, Sara's brother. You won't want to come home with me yet, will you?"

"No, Dad."

I don't know how I managed to take the next breath. It's not easy when the world has just turned upside down and inside out. Dad, Dad, he's her Dad.

"I'll just have a word with Margaret before I go. See you again," he nodded and left. She was grinning at me.

"He's all right," she said.

I managed to nod. The world was slowly returning to something near normal, though this was a pretty shattering evening. I sat down weakly next to her.

"Your sister's very beautiful," she said.

"I think you are," I said, full of courage.

"No, I'm funny-looking. Everyone says so."

"I don't. Sal's supposed to be coming if you want to speak to her."

"She's there. Look."

Sal had come in through the french windows at the other side of the room. Beautiful? She looked like old Sal, mack pulled in tight, not as fat as she used to be and pale, too many late nights, as Ma would say. And just behind loomed Oliver and Kenny.

Anger broke over me like the Severn spring tide, filling me so that I could hardly breathe. Were those two always going to be around? Why didn't they leave me in peace? Why didn't they get off my back? Get off my back, will you? And take your wretched stuff with you when you go. They were coming over. I didn't want them speaking to Midge. I didn't want to hear blasted Oliver's sneering Peterkin in his snobby up-market voice.

So "Excuse me," I said and walked towards them.

"Welcoming us home, then?" smiled Oliver. I'll remember that smile when I'm ninety. "Your Ma worked the miracle. She's our guarantee for good conduct."

Kenny broke the habit of a lifetime and uttered, "Good ole Ma."

So I hit him. Just on the side of the jaw as my Dad showed me years ago, trying to get me to stand up for myself. He went down like a log, stirred, tried to get up and I hit him again. Hard. There were shouts and screams all about me. I didn't care . . .

"And now for you . . . you . . ."

But Oliver wasn't waiting for his trade description — he backed away, hands gesticulating, smiling, smiling . . .

"Cool it, Pete. You've got it all wrong . . ."

Sal was trying to hold me, but I pushed her off.

"No, I haven't got it wrong you sponging, blackmailing bastard. You got me wrong and I'm putting it right!"

He was at the french windows now, and within my grip. Suddenly he whipped through them and crashed them back against me, and my head butted into the frame. Pain, blackness, sick . . . and far away a voice, no it couldn't be.

"There are police outside, wanting someone called . . . What is this? Pete, what have you been doing now? I blame your mother. Where are you, Magsie? Sybil? . . . What about that old ratbag . . . ?"

It couldn't be but it was. My father had arrived.

A horn blasts like the sound of the Last Trump. My father is driving like a bat out of hell, and the girl holds me, saying does it hurt, does it hurt? I don't want you to hurt.

Lights everywhere.

"Not all of you. Please." I focus very clear.

A tall, dishy nurse with Brooke Shields eyebrows smiles at me and I can speak.

"Am I dying?"

"No, I shouldn't think so. You're living."

So that's what they call it.

8

Dad loomed in the doorway and the smell of burning meat wafted through the house. Dad was speaking.

"I leave the ancestral home to earn a dishonest crust for my ungrateful family, then full of desire to see them I drive for hours in diabolical conditions to sample all those comforts so dear to me to find what? You may well ask. The house looking like an inner city demolition job, broken glasses, broken windows, broken bodies, people screaming, idiots everywhere, Pete a star casualty, police swarming all over the place, Sybil's revolting house burgled — a fair redistribution of wealth, in her case, one could say — Willie's Gran's done over — disgusting — Pete's mates arrested, which was only a matter of time. Didn't you all do well? I blame your mother. And you, naturally. Just what were you up to when I came in? Suicide? Training for circus work? Creating a new Art form?"

"I lost my temper," I muttered.

"Splendid. I'd begun to think you hadn't got one."

Ma came in.

"Are we roasting the fatted calf for my return, Magsie?"

"No, it's the meat burning. I forgot it, working out the synopsis for my new book, but it'll be no worse than usual."

"What's the new masterpiece about?"

"Teenage problems."

"That'll be fun. I can't wait to read it. Any more thrilling news?"

"Oh, yes, Wreford and I discussed Peter . . ."

"Oh, no," I groaned, but funnily enough, it didn't seem to be important any more, or else I'd gone beyond caring.

". . . and he thinks Peter has a most original mind. No one else thought of not filling in the test paper. It didn't occur to them."

"No, it wouldn't. There aren't many about like him. Totally mad."

My head hurt, and this conversation was making it worse.

"Shut up, Dad," I growled. They looked at me in surprise. "I can't help it if Ma talks rubbish about me. And you do, Ma, and it's awful. And another thing. If I'm thick and wet, you'll just have to put up with it. It's what I'm like. I'm not going to try to change any more and go in for all that aggro stuff. It's not me, and besides it didn't work, did it? Look at the state I'm in."

Through the door came Sal, carrying a box of chocolates, and then Midge, almost lost behind a bunch of flowers. Verna and Claire grinned from the doorway with a pile of paperbacks.

"You must be joking," said my father.

Oliver got six months and Kenny three, for shoplifting, and breaking and entering Willie's house. The gang, the big fish, were picked up later. Oliver and Kenny had never really been involved in any jobs with them, nor had they planted drugs in our house. It was Oliver's invention to keep Willie and me running; petty stuff.

Midge wasn't quite the shy maiden of my dreams, no. She turned out to be the College's outstanding student in Maths and computer studies and a judo expert, but that was nice as she helped me with my Maths and I felt safe when we went out at night.

Nick and Verna had a mad, crazy affair, with rows, battles and power struggles going on all the time. Claire continued to

116

fancy Willie, and Willie Sal, and in the meantime go out with each other.

Oliver's people never went near him while he was in prison, but Kenny's mother visited Kenny whenever she could. Ma, of course, visited them both.

The first time she was setting out, Sal gave her an envelope to give to Oliver.

"Well, yes, but what for?" Ma asked. A dreadful suspicion crept over me as Sal went red, then white.

"I fancy him. That's what for. And I want to write to him while he's in . . . in there."

Ma sat down and looked green.

"But my dear Sara, he's a dreadful person," she cried, admitting it at last. "Not you, not . . ."

"Sara, the Wonder Horse?" She grinned at me. "Isn't it time I put a foot wrong, at last? And if I can't manage him, who can?"

But Ma rallied. She's like that.

"Let me see. You'd better read law, if you can get in. Then you'll be able to organize his defence whenever he gets into trouble. That's the answer. Good, I'm glad that's settled."

MARTINI-ON-THE-ROCKS AND OTHER STORIES
Susan Gregory

Eight very funny, chaotic, true-to-life stories about a bunch of typical teenagers. They fall in love, get into trouble, cheat, tease, laugh, and are very, very lively. Anybody who's ever been to school cannot fail to be entertained!

BROTHER IN THE LAND
Robert Swindells

Which is worse – to perish in a nuclear attack, or to survive? Danny has no choice. He and his young brother Ben have come through the holocaust alive, only to discover that the world has gone sour in more ways than one. Survival depends on being able to live on your wits, outsmarting the rest and fighting to protect your home and family. But when the authorities finally put in an appearance, help is the last thing they bring.

A PARCEL OF PATTERNS
Jill Paton Walsh

It is Mall who tells of the tragedy of the fearful plague coming to her village, possibly brought from London by a parcel of dress patterns. She tells dramatically and powerfully how the villagers lived and died, and their collective heroism in containing the disease. But this is also a moving love-story, for Mall must not go to meet her beloved Thomas, for fear of passing the sickness on to him.

EASY CONNECTIONS
Liz Berry

Some people say Cathy is a brilliant painter with an exceptional future ahead of her. But from the day when she unwittingly trespasses on the country estate of rock star Paul Devlin, she becomes a changed character. Beautiful, cold and violent, Dev is captivated by Cathy, while she is attracted and repelled in equal measures. However, Dev usually gets what he wants . . . An unusual love story set in the vivid worlds of rock music and art.

IF IT WEREN'T FOR SEBASTIAN . . .
Jean Ure

Maggie's decision to break the family tradition of studying science at university in favour of a course in shorthand-typing causes a major row. But the rift with her parents is nothing to the difficulties she meets when unpredictable Sebastian enters her life.

SWEET FRANNIE
Susan Sallis

Confined to a wheel-chair, Fran doesn't seem to have much of a future. But then Luke Hawkins moves into the same residential home and who better to help him adjust to the loss of his legs in a road accident? A touching but unsentimental story.

THE DISAPPEARANCE
Rosa Guy

Only two days after Imamu came to live with the Aimsleys, their small daughter has disappeared. Just charged (and acquitted) on a murder rap, the 16-year-old Harlem boy hasn't won his foster-family's trust yet. Did he have anything to do with Perk's disappearance? Maybe Gail's determination and Imamu's street wisdom will solve a mystery the police aren't too interested in.

EDITH JACKSON
Rosa Guy

Orphans always find each other, and when Mrs Bates found 17-year-old Edith Jackson desperately trying to hold the remnants of a family together, she recognized her own past. She too had struggled against the handicap of being poor, black, female and an orphan, but she knew that until Edith herself decided that she was a person who could make choices and fight for them, she wouldn't begin to count.

HIGH PAVEMENT BLUES
Bernard Ashley

Kevin lives with his mum, helping out on her leather stall in the market at weekends. For him, Saturday is the worst day of the week because that's when he has to set up the stall on his own and put up with the aggravation from Alfie Cox on the stall next door. At times, Kevin would give anything for a bit more family support, but it's only when he meets Karen that he decides to do something about it . . .

A PROPER LITTLE NOORYEFF
Jean Ure

Jamie was a fool. A dolt. A clod. A weak-kneed, lily-livered yellow-bellied clod. Why couldn't he say no? It was all his sister Kim's fault: she was just crazy about ballet and if she hadn't insisted that he meet her after her classes he'd still be playing cricket for his school instead of prancing about in a pair of tights. And what if the mob from Tenterden Road Comprehensive found out?

THE VILLAGE BY THE SEA
Anita Desai

Hari and his sister Lila are the eldest children of an Indian family. Their mother is ill and their father spends most of his time in a drunken stupor. Grimly, Lila and Hari struggle to hold the family together until one day, in a last-ditch attempt to break out of this poverty, Hari leaves his sisters in the silent, shadowy hut and runs away to Bombay. How Hari and Lila cope with the harsh realities of life in city and village is vividly described in this moving and powerful story.

A FOREIGN AFFAIR
John Rowe Townsend

It doesn't seem like a promising party, but when the best-looking boy in the room – the Crown Prince of Essenheim – seeks her out, Kate is flattered. But it comes as a blow when he appears equally interested in her father, a political journalist. On hearing rumours of an impending revolution in Essenheim, Kate begins to understand Rudi's dual motive, but little dreams that she too has a vital part to play in the future of that country. A funny and fast paced story about affairs of state and affairs of the heart!

THE WIND EYE

Bertrand and Madeleine shouldn't have got married. Even their children seemed to think so – though the children themselves got on as well as any half-brothers and sisters could be expected to. Their holiday together got off to a bad start when Madeleine trampled on St Cuthbert's tomb in Durham Cathedral. From then on, the eye of the long-dead saint was well and truly on them . . .

FUTURETRACK 5

Henry Kitson lives in the twenty-first century, where success is determined by being good – not too good – and by a willingness to conform. Those who don't make it are consigned through the Wire, lobotomized or, in Kitson's case, allocated to Tech – a small body of people who maintain the computers. Meeting bike champion Keri is a turning point for Kitson, and the two form an uneasy alliance to find out just what makes the system tick.

LET THE CIRCLE BE UNBROKEN
Mildred D. Taylor

For Cassie Logan, 1935 in the American deep south is a time of bewildering change: the Depression is tightening its grip, rich and poor are in conflict and racial tension is increasing. As she grows away from the security of childhood, Cassie struggles to understand the turmoil around her and the reasons for the deep-rooted fears of her family and friends.